SWEET LIES AND RAINBOW SKIES

SWEET LIES AND RAINBOW SKIES

•

JANE MCBRIDE CHOATE

AVALON BOOKS
THOMAS BOUREGY AND COMPANY, INC.
401 LAFAYETTE STREET
NEW YORK, NEW YORK 10003

PRINTED IN THE UNITED STATES OF AMERICA
ON ACID-FREE PAPER
BY HADDON CRAFTSMEN, SCRANTON, PENNSYLVANIA

To: Alanna, Robert, Steven, Hyrum, and Ann

You are the rainbows in my life

Chapter One

"Boss? You about ready to knock off? Me and the boys were wondering if you'd like to have a beer with us tonight."

Clint Bradley looked up at Charlie Owens just as his foreman swiped at his forehead with a sweat-stained kerchief. For the first time that day, Clint's smile was genuine. Charlie was one of the old-timers who'd been with Clint from the beginning. He'd been both father and friend.

"Thanks, Charlie, but not tonight. I've still got to go over these contracts. They're supposed to be in the mail tomorrow."

Charlie shuffled from one foot to the other. "Sure, Boss. Another time."

"Thanks, Charlie."

1

"Yeah, sure."

Clint scrubbed a hand against his jaw and glanced at the papers in front of him one last time. The figures blurred before his eyes, evidence of too many late nights and too little sleep.

When the shift ended, Clint personally handed out the paychecks. He summoned a smile as the men filed past. Many of them had been with him when the business had consisted of little more than a twenty-year-old pickup and a secondhand set of tools. Sweat and a burning desire to make his dream of Bradley Construction come true had provided the rest.

Bending over the stack of papers on his desk, he reached for a mug of coffee, took a gulp, and grimaced. It tasted like sludge, but he forced himself to drink it. He needed the jolt of caffeine. If he didn't get these contracts finished, he'd miss the deadline. He frowned. When had signing contracts and meeting deadlines become the sum total of his existence?

He ignored the question and slogged through the paperwork, determined to complete the unpleasant task before he left that night. Another frown creased his forehead as he thought of the house that was to have been a home.

Without enthusiasm, he drove to the stone and glass monstrosity he was to have shared with Sherry. He hadn't been able to bring himself to think of it as home, even though he'd built it himself. An ironic smile creased his lips as he remembered his fiancée's list of what she wanted in their dream house.

It was a dream all right . . . a nightmare of marble columns and fountains with cupids. It made about as much sense in its natural setting nestled in the Denver foothills as did anything else in his life right now.

He still remembered his shock when Sherry had casually ended their engagement.

"It's a chance of a lifetime," she said, handing the diamond ring back to Clint. "Working with one of the top fashion designers in London. You can't expect me to give it up."

"I guess I can't," he agreed, not surprised that she failed to pick up on his sarcasm.

She waved good-bye with scarcely a backward glance. Her desertion hadn't bothered Clint nearly as much as the fact that he felt so little when she returned his ring. Whatever had brought them together in the first place clearly no longer mattered. When he stopped to think about it, they'd shared little more than traveling in the same social circles in Denver society. He'd been lucky, he decided.

With Sherry gone, he'd spent more hours than ever at the office, digging himself further into a business that had grown faster than he'd ever dreamed.

An ironic smile twisted his mouth as he thought of the years he'd spent building the business into one of the most respected and admired outfits in Denver. He was good with his hands. It turned out he was equally good with his brains, as more and more of his duties consisted of the seemingly endless paperwork necessary to operate a business the size of Bradley Construction.

Idly, Clint noticed his hands. They were smooth, almost soft, more accustomed to signing checks and negotiating contracts than they were to manual labor. There'd been a time when his palms were ridged with callouses, the knuckles skinned and bruised, the fingernails embedded with dirt.

His life, he decided, was as superficial as the tone of his muscles, which were hard not from *work*, but from *workouts* at one of Denver's prestigious health clubs.

There'd been a time, he mused, when he had a sense of purpose. Somewhere along the line, he'd lost that. Securing loans, bidding on contracts, wining and dining clients had replaced working with his hands, creating something of beauty. He'd been grateful for his success, but it had cost him.

Now he wondered if the price had been too great. Lately, he'd found little pleasure or enjoyment in his work. Pride in building something of lasting value had been sacrificed in favor of success. Hunched over a desk in the den, the one room he'd refused to let Sherry have professionally decorated, he propped his chin on his hands and tried to remember when he last had a good night's sleep.

He couldn't.

He needed time away from the business to try to figure where his life had gone wrong. He shivered.

Despite the heat of the late September day, he was cold.

Time away.

The idea appealed to him more than he thought possible, but he pushed it away. He had too many responsibilities, too many people depending upon him. Again, he thrust the idea out of his mind. But it refused to stay buried.

He'd done it.

Two days later, Clint glanced around his house. Dust cloths shrouded the furniture. He'd stopped delivery of the mail and paper. Only Charlie Owens knew of his plan. He'd made no attempt to talk Clint out of it.

He grinned, feeling better than he had in months. Maybe years. He was no longer Clinton Bradley, president and owner of Bradley Construction. He was . . . He grinned again. He was plain Clint Bradley.

He stashed a small amount of cash in the bottom of his duffel bag. Once last glance around assured him he wasn't leaving anything behind. Nothing important anyway.

Pink fingers of light poked their way through the darkness as he headed out of the city. Even at this hour, traffic inched its way along. As he drove farther south, the sky, freed from its burden of smog, grew lighter, the air fresher.

He didn't know where he was going, only that he needed to find a place where he could start to breathe again. Whether it was fate or just plain luck, he didn't know. He didn't much care. A sign saying Last Stop, Colorado, loomed in front of him. He swerved onto the off ramp.

Last Stop was small, as its name suggested. Flower beds flanked the town square, which boasted a statue of a long-forgotten war hero. Clapboard houses lined the streets, their pastel colors set off by pristine white shutters. A family town, he decided approvingly.

He drove aimlessly, not sure what he was looking for until he saw the dog lying in the highway. He jumped out of the car and knelt by the dog, relieved to find it still breathing. Gently, he lifted the mutt and carried it back to the truck. He scanned the area as he drove, looking for help.

He discovered he'd driven beyond the town limits, where the houses were fewer. A weather-beaten house with peeling yellow paint and a sad-looking picket fence caught his attention. He pulled into a gravel driveway.

A sharp rap on the door stirred Brittany from her reverie. Andy was resting, and she had drifted off into a pleasant daydream where there were no money problems, no painful memories that shadowed her days and haunted her nights.

Opening the door, she found a man holding a brown and white dog in his arms. Blood spurted from a gash in the mutt's side.

"I found this poor fellow by the side of the road. Looks like he's been run over. Can I use your phone and call a vet?"

She reached for a towel and watched as he pressed it against the wound. "I'm sorry. We don't have a phone yet. But I can drive you to the vet's. He lives a couple of miles down the road."

"Thanks."

She bundled a white-faced Andy into the front seat of the ancient Volkswagen. The stranger, still holding the mutt, slid into the back seat. Though he continued compressing the towel against the wound, blood spurted out.

"I'm afraid we're getting blood all over the car."

She shot him a glance in the rearview mirror. "It's been through worse. I hope he's going to be all right."

"So do I." His lips tightened. "I'd like to have five minutes alone with the creep who ran down a helpless animal and then left him to die."

She stole a look at him, trying to make sense of the contradictory impressions she was receiving. From the set of his mouth, she guessed he was holding his temper under a tight rein. She wouldn't want to cross this man, she decided. But his concern for the hurt animal tempered the harsh line of his lips.

"How much farther?" he demanded.

"Not much." She pulled onto a dirt road. "At the end of this lane." The elderly car creaked and groaned over the rutted road. She swerved sharply into a driveway that was little more than a furrowed strip of dirt. "We're here."

Before she'd completely stopped, the man was

climbing out of the car. He carried the dog inside. Brittany and Andy followed.

"Jim," she called. "It's Brittany Howard."

"Coming," a voice answered from an inner room. A youngish man appeared. Still drying his hands on a towel, he stopped short at the sight of Clint holding the injured dog.

"In here." Jim Roberts ushered them into the small operating room. He grimaced as he removed the towel. "Someone really did a number on him."

"Yeah. Think you can fix him up?"

The doctor glanced at Brittany, who whispered something to Andy. "We'll wait for you out here."

"What about it, Doc?" Clint asked.

"I don't know." The vet examined the mangled leg. "I can't promise anything, but I'll give it my best shot."

"That's all I ask."

The doctor looked at Clint. "Are you a friend of Brittany's?"

"Just met her today. I found the dog by the side of the road and took him to her place. She offered to drive us here."

Doctor Roberts smiled. "That sounds like Brittany. She can't stand to see anyone, or anything, suffer."

"Do you want us to wait?"

"No sense in that. I'll be a couple of hours at least."

"Can I come back then?"

"I'll call you."

Clint hesitated. "I don't have a phone. I'm sort of

between jobs at the moment, and looking for a place to stay.''

The doctor gave him an assessing look. ''I'll drive out to Brittany's place and let her know. That all right with you?''

''Yeah, sure.'' Clint paused on his way out. ''Thanks, Doc.''

Already involved in cleaning the wound, the vet waved him away.

Clint found Brittany and Andy waiting in front room. ''He says it'll be a couple of hours before we know anything.''

''Aunt Brittany, is the dog going to be all right?'' Andy asked the question that hovered in the air.

She hugged him to her. ''We don't know yet. I'm sure the doctor will do everything he can. But sometimes there are hurts that can't be fixed.''

''Can I catch a ride back with you to my truck?'' Clint asked.

''Of course.''

A subdued little group, they piled in the car.

He broke the silence as they neared her house. ''Thanks for the lift to the vet's.''

''I'm glad I could help. What will happen to the poor thing if Jim manages to patch him up?''

''We'll have to find his owner. If that fails, then I suppose an animal shelter will take him.''

''But that's where—'' She broke off, not willing to put the possibilities into words, especially in front of Andy.

Clint didn't look any happier than she did. "Yeah."

Andy shifted in his seat. "Aunt Brittany?"

Grateful to change the subject, she smiled at him. "What, honey?"

"If the doctor can make him better, can we keep him?"

She should have known. She darted a look at the stranger and saw a smile twitching at his lips. "There's probably someone looking for him now, Andy."

"But if there's not?" he persisted.

"We'll have to see," she temporized. "Dogs need a lot of care and love. They have to be fed and walked and all sorts of things."

"I could do that. Please."

She ruffled his hair. "We can't decide anything until we see if Jim can make him well. Then *if*," she stressed, "*if* someone else doesn't claim him, we might—"

She wasn't able to finish the sentence as Andy let out a shout. "Whoopee. We're going to have a dog."

Brittany felt the man's gaze on her. She gave him a rueful smile which he returned.

"Sorry," he whispered over Andy's head. "I didn't realize what I was getting you into."

"That's all right. I'm glad you found him." She pulled the car into the driveway and hesitated before getting out. "Are you hungry?"

"A little."

"We're just having franks and beans, but you're

welcome to join us.'' The invitation came before she could stop herself.

He looked at the porch rail. ''How about if I fix this in return for the meal?''

''If you want.''

Why had she asked him to stay? Something in the way he looked, perhaps. And his compassion for a hurt animal.

''By the way, the name's Clint Bradley.''

''Brittany Howard,'' she said, extending her hand and finding it swallowed by his.

He held it no longer than was necessary. ''Pleased to meet you, Mrs. Howard.''

''It's Miss,'' she corrected. ''Andy's my nephew.''

''Miss Howard,'' he said. ''If you'd show me where your tool box is . . .''

She led him to the kitchen and pulled out a long, narrow drawer. ''Any tools I have are in here.'' She gestured toward the haphazard assortment.

''Looks like you need a few of the more basic tools,'' he said, picking up a hammer with a broken handle.

She had to agree. ''You're right. There've just been so many things . . .''

He touched her lightly on the shoulder. ''Don't worry about it. I'll make do.''

''Dinner'll be in half an hour.''

''Great.'' He looked like he wanted to say something more. Instead, he said only, ''I'd better get busy.''

He smiled, and she found herself returning it. Annoyed that she should respond to him, she turned her back and busied herself at the stove. Mechanically, she began preparing dinner, rinsing and chopping vegetables for a salad, mixing up a cake.

Already, she regretted her impulse to invite him to stay to dinner. What had she been thinking? Still, she couldn't have turned him away. She could never turn away someone who shared her compassion for the hurt, helpless things of the world.

"In about thirty minutes then," she said in dismissal, her voice intentionally cool.

Working methodically, Clint fixed the porch railing with little more than a few nails and the broken hammer. He kept his thoughts at bay by blanking his mind to everything but the task at hand. He swore silently when he hit his finger with the wobbly hammer.

A scuffling sound alerted him to the fact that he was no longer alone. Turning around, he found a pair of curious gray eyes peering at him. He took the time to study the small boy before him. Red-gold hair framed a face lightly dotted with freckles. Miniature jeans topped by a rugby shirt clothed a slight body. He'd noted the leg braces before, but he didn't wince at the sight of them.

He squatted down so that they were at eye level. "My name's Clint, remember? Yours is Andy, right?"

The small boy didn't answer, his current shyness contrasting with his excitement of a few minutes earlier.

At that moment, Brittany reappeared. "Mr. Bradley,

would you like to wash up?'' She glanced from Andy to the man and back again. ''You too, Andy.''

''Right behind you,'' Clint said.

Together, the three of them enjoyed the meal of hot dogs, baked beans, salad, and cake.

To Brittany's surprise, Andy opened up under Clint's gentle attention and laughed more in that one evening than he had in the previous six weeks since they'd moved to Last Stop. For that alone, she was grateful to Clint.

He must have read some of her feelings in her eyes, for he smiled back.

Unexpectedly, she wished the evening could continue, but she knew Andy was tired, even though he denied it. Glancing at her watch, Brittany caught Clint's attention.

Feigning a yawn, he smiled sheepishly. ''Guess I'm a little tired.''

She flashed him a grateful look. When Andy would have protested, she bent down to brush a kiss against his forehead. ''Off to bed. I'll tuck you in in a few minutes.''

''Aw, Aunt Brittany.''

She swatted his bottom. ''Scoot.''

''Okay.'' He scuffled off.

Brittany surreptitiously studied the man seated across from her. In spite of jeans turned white at the stress points and chambray work shirt, he didn't give the impression of an ordinary handyman. She wasn't sure why she should feel that way. Certainly, the powerful muscles barely concealed by his shirt hinted at a man accustomed to physical labor.

Could she . . . ? She shook her head. She didn't know him. Still, he appeared to be down on his luck and in need of a job. Maybe . . .

She was a woman who went by her emotions. All her intuition told her that Clint Bradley was a man who could be trusted. And she needed help. A lot of the repairs that needed to be done around the house required two people, or at least someone stronger than herself.

"Look, Mr. Bradley," Brittany said when Andy was out of earshot, "you seem to know your way around tools, and I need some help getting this place in shape. If you're interested, you've got yourself a job. I couldn't pay much, maybe a little more than minimum wage. How does five dollars an hour sound?"

He gave her an incredulous look. "Let me get this straight. You're offering me a job?"

"Yes."

"As a handyman?"

"If you like." He continued to look at her, until she rushed on. "I know the pay's not much, but maybe later, if things work out, we could make it a bit more." A thought occurred to her. "Do you have a place to stay?"

"No."

"We could throw in room and board."

Still, he hesitated.

"If it's the salary," she began.

"It's not that."

"What is it?"

"It's been a long time since I've worked as a handyman," he said slowly.

She smiled at him. "There's no shame in being out of a job. Lots of people are out of work these days."

"Can I ask you a question?"

"Sure."

"Why me?"

She hunched a shoulder. "I don't know. Maybe it's the way you cared about the dog. Or how you were with Andy. It's been a long time since he's had a man pay attention to him. I'd forgotten how much that can mean to a little boy."

She watched as he shifted awkwardly in his chair and added, "I don't mean he'd be underfoot. Only that having you around would be good for him. If you'd rather not—"

"I accept."

"You do? That's great. I'm afraid there's not an extra bedroom, but you could sleep in the barn."

"I always did like the smell of hay."

A sound in the hallway alerted her that they were no longer alone. Brittany looked up to find Andy standing in the hall.

"Aunt Brittany, is Mr. Bradley going to stay?"

She looked at Clint, who nodded. "For a while."

Andy limped toward them. "Maybe you can help me take care of Ralph, Mr. Bradley."

"Ralph?" Both Clint and Brittany asked at once.

"My dog."

Brittany felt a smile tugging at her lips. "That's a good name for a dog." She crossed the room to kneel down in front of him. "But we don't know if he'll get better or if we'll get to keep him," she reminded him gently. "Don't get your hopes up, honey."

His face fell, and Brittany hugged him. "But Dr. Jim is awfully smart. I'm sure he'll find a way to make Ralph better."

"Yeah. And if his owners don't show up . . . "

"Tomorrow, Andy," Clint broke in, "maybe you can help me fix the porch steps. How about it?"

Andy turned to Brittany. "Can I?"

"If you're sure he won't get in your way, that'll be fine," she said, her gaze seeking Clint's.

"He'll be my number one helper. And, by the way, it's Clint. Okay?"

"All right. And make it Brittany."

He smiled, a slow, chipped-tooth smile.

They held each other's gaze for a moment longer before she dropped her own. Something passed between them. She wasn't sure what. She wasn't sure if she wanted to know.

Chapter Two

The ping of a hammer woke her. She pushed her hair back from her face and glanced at the clock. Six o'clock.

Resisting the temptation to burrow back under the covers, she scrambled from the bed, threw a robe around her shoulders, and followed the sound to the front porch.

"'Morning, Brittany."

"G'morning, Clint. It's a little early, isn't it?"

He checked his watch. "Sorry. Did I wake you?"

"Oh, no. I'm always up at dawn." She smothered a yawn.

He gave her an apologetic look. "Sorry," he said again. "I couldn't sleep and thought I'd get an early start."

"Now I'm the one who's sorry. I should have known you wouldn't be comfortable in the barn. Maybe we could—"

"No. I mean, it wasn't that. The barn's fine."

"If you're sure."

"I'm sure."

He looked around. "There's a lot to be done."

She followed his gaze. "When the real estate agent said fixer-upper, he wasn't exaggerating."

Clint chuckled. "I'm afraid not. But it's got a lot going for it. The house is basically sound. So's the barn."

The chilly fingers of early morning trickled through her robe, and she shivered.

Clint frowned. "You're cold."

"No," she said and negated the denial as she trembled again. "I'm fine." She hesitated. "I . . . I'd better go start breakfast. I hope you like pancakes."

"Buttermilk?"

She grinned. "Is there any other kind?"

Inside, she quickly pulled off her gown and slipped into the shower. Five minutes later, she was tugging on jeans and a shirt.

Brittany hummed softly while mixing the pancakes.

"I haven't heard you sing in a long time," Andy said.

She stopped. "You're right. I guess I haven't." *There's not been much to sing about.* "What if we sing a song you know? How about 'It's a Small World'?"

She started in with Andy chirping along. They sang loudly, if not on key.

A round of applause startled her, and she swung around to find Clint watching them.

"Encore. Encore."

Blushing, she turned back to the sink. "You must think we're crazy."

"No way. I figured I was getting a freebie—music with my breakfast."

She gave a wry smile. "If I don't get this batter mixed, there won't be any breakfast."

"Mind if I wash up here?"

"Sure." Brittany watched as he rolled up his sleeves, fascinated with the sprinkling of light brown hair that covered his arms. Forcibly, she returned her attention to the bowl of batter in front of her.

He turned the cold water on and held his left hand under it. "The hammer and I had an argument. It won." He held up his hand and showed a blackened thumb nail.

She dropped the wooden spoon she'd been using. "I'm sorry. It's my fault for giving you those crummy tools."

"Hey. It's nobody's fault." He gave a crooked smile. "I've survived worse."

Somehow she believed that. "Can I get you anything? A bandage or something?"

He dried his hands on a dish towel. "I'll be fine."

They ate companionably, Clint and Andy putting away six pancakes apiece.

"That was delicious," Clint said, pushing his chair away from the table.

Unaccountably pleased with the simple praise, Brittany mumbled her thanks. She started clearing the table. He rose to help her.

"You don't have to."

"I want to."

She scraped the dishes after he handed them to her.

The doorbell chimed, and Andy shuffled to answer it. "Aunt Brittany, it's Doctor Roberts. Hurry up," he urged when she didn't immediately respond. "Hey, Clint, the vet's here."

She held up crossed fingers. "I hope it's good news."

Clint wiped his hands on his jeans and followed her into the living room.

Brittany smiled. "Hi, Jim."

Jim Roberts held a battered hat in his hand; an equally battered tan corduroy jacket was slung over one shoulder. "Sorry I didn't get out last night. Two more emergencies came up after you left." He glanced about. "Hope I'm not interrupting."

"Not at all. I'm glad you stopped by. How's Ralph?"

At Jim's perplexed look, she laughed self-consciously and explained, "That's what Andy named him. I guess I started thinking of him as Ralph too."

A slow grin stretched across the vet's face. "Ralph. I like it. Well, Ralph is going to be fine. A couple days' rest and he'll be good as new. He'll have to stay where I can watch him for a little longer, but then he can go home.''

"Ralph's going to be all right," Andy shouted. "Yeah, Andy, he is. But he won't be able to play with you for a while yet," Jim warned. He looked around and frowned at Clint, who leaned against a wall. "See you're still here, Bradley."

Clint met the other man's measuring gaze with one of his own. "Yeah. Miss Howard's offered me a job fixing up the place."

"Oh." Jim appeared suddenly ill at ease. "Are you figuring on keeping Ralph, Brittany?"

"I don't know. Andy's got his heart set on it. Of course, if the owner shows up . . . " She spread her hands. "Can I talk you into a cup of coffee?"

"Sounds good." He wiped his mud-caked feet on the mat. "I just came from the Janzens' place," he said in explanation. "Old Tess has mastitis again."

Clint raised his eyebrows.

"Tess is their milk cow," Brittany explained.

"Gets mastitis about once a month." At her disbelieving look, Jim smiled. "Seems like that anyway."

Andy tugged at her hand. "Can we keep him? Can we keep Ralph?"

She made a waiting motion before turning to Jim. "What happens to him now?"

"It's hard to say. Sometimes an owner shows up to claim an animal. But, more often than not, no one comes at all. In that case, he'll go to the animal shelter."

Andy's lip trembled.

"Would there be any problem in letting Andy take care of him here?" Clint asked. "Until his owner shows up?"

"No problem at all. In fact, that takes a load off my mind. I hate sending animals to the shelter. But there's no way I can keep them all."

"How soon can he come live with us?" Andy asked.

"Maybe another day or two." Jim flashed a smile at Brittany. "I'd better be going. Just wanted to let you know he's going to be fine."

"Thanks for coming by." A flicker of concern crossed her face. "About the fee, Jim."

"Forget it. Consider it my contribution to Andy's new friend."

She smiled her thanks at him. "That's sweet of you, but I can't let you do that. You'll be broke in a week if you run your business like that."

"How about if Andy and I work off the bill?" Clint suggested. "Since I was the one who found him, I feel sort of responsible for Ralph too." When no one answered, he persisted, "We could clean out cages, feed the animals, whatever needs done. What do you say, Andy?"

"Great."

Brittany looked at Jim Roberts, who nodded.

"Looks like I've got two helpers." Jim checked his watch. "I'd better be on my way. I've got to check on the Willets' mare. She's in labor."

"We'll be out this afternoon if that's all right with you, Doc," Clint said.

"Can I see Ralph then?" Andy asked.

"Sure thing."

Brittany walked Jim to the door. "Thanks for agreeing to let Clint and Andy help out."

Jim steered her out the door, then carefully closed it behind them. "Who is this Clint Bradley, Brittany? Where'd he come from?"

"Just someone down on his luck. He's going to do some repairs for me."

"You think it's safe letting a perfect stranger move in like that?"

"Usually, no. But he's down on his luck, and he cared about Ralph, and Andy likes him." She gave an embarrassed laugh. "That sounds pretty stupid, doesn't it?"

Jim patted her shoulder. "No. Just be careful. Okay?"

"Okay."

She turned around to find Clint watching her.

"Jim seems like a decent sort."

"He is," she agreed, and waited. He seemed about to say something more.

"I'd better get to work on the porch steps. I promised Andy we'd start after breakfast. Ready, Andy?"

"You bet."

Brittany watched as Andy followed Clint outside and wished she could join them. Reluctantly, she looked at the stack of papers on her desk. She still had papers to grade plus her lesson plan to go over.

Two hours later, she pushed her lesson plan away and rubbed the back of her neck. Her shoulders ached, and she rotated them experimentally.

"Aunt Brittany, is lunch ready?"

She turned to find Andy watching her.

"Clint said you were busy and not to bother you, but I'm hungry." He rubbed his stomach in emphasis.

"That's all right. I'm finished."

"All right if we barge in now?" Clint asked.

She smiled. "Sure. And thanks for the quiet. I've been putting this off." She pointed to the neatly stacked papers.

"Paperwork?"

"I was going over lesson plans for a little boy I tutor."

"Do you do private tutoring?"

"Some. I also work at the school, giving special help to kids who need it. Robbie doesn't go to school, so I go to his home."

"Why doesn't he go to school like other kids?"

"He has a learning disability. His father thinks he'll do better . . . without a lot of distractions."

"I see."

"Robbie's so lonely. He needs to be around other children. But his father can't see that. That's why I've been putting this off—my heart isn't in it. I've been trying to convince Mr. Tolley to let Robbie attend school."

"You care about your students."

She nodded, self-conscious at how much she'd revealed about herself. "I hate to see a child suffering. And Robbie is. Not physically, but emotionally." She flushed, embarrassed at her rambling. "I'll have lunch ready in a few minutes if you two want to wash up."

Lunch was a hurried meal with Andy practically jumping up and down with impatience.

"Is it time?" Andy demanded for the tenth time as Brittany finished cleaning up.

She checked her watch. "Almost." She smiled at her nephew, who was more excited than she'd ever seen him.

Ten minutes later, they all piled into the Volkswagen.

"What are you going to do while we clean out cages?" Clint asked.

"I'm going over to the Tolleys' house. I'm usually there about two hours."

At the clinic, Jim yelled for them to have a seat. "Sorry about that," he said when he appeared a few minutes later. "I had a German shepherd getting his nails clipped." He gave the dog a pat on the rump as his owner led him away.

"Bradley, you and Andy can start in the storeroom." He pointed to the back of the office. "I'm trying to clean it out so I can make more room for my patients."

"You mean we can't work with the animals?" Andy asked, clearly disappointed.

"I think Andy wanted to help clean their cages," Clint said.

"If that's what you really want, you're welcome to it," Jim said. "It's a messy job."

"Hey, we're not afraid of a little mess, are we, buddy?" Clint patted Andy's shoulder.

"No way."

Clint turned back to Jim. "If you'll show us what we're supposed to do, Doctor, we'll get at it."

"I'll pick you guys up after my lesson with Robbie. Does a couple of hours sound all right?" Brittany asked Jim.

"Sounds fine. Let me show them what to do and I'll be right back," Jim said.

"Fine. I'll look at your pictures." Jim's office was lined with pictures of his patients.

He returned within a few minutes, a troubled look in his eyes.

"Brittany, I know you like this guy, but—"

"Don't start," she warned. "Clint's a nice man who's a little down on his luck. If you'd seen him with Andy this morning—"

"That's just the point. I *saw* him with Andy. Andy's got a king-size case of hero worship. What's going to happen when Bradley moves on? You did say he was a drifter, didn't you?"

"Not exactly. But what can it hurt for a little boy to have someone to look up to? He hasn't had much of that in his life."

"I know it's been rough for you." A caressing note

entered his voice. "If you'd let me, we could change that."

"Jim, I care about you. As a friend. Let's keep it that way, at least for now. Okay?"

He gave her a rueful smile. "I don't have much choice, do I? But there's something about that guy. I can't put my finger on it, but something doesn't ring true."

She lifted her chin.

He held up a hand. "All right. I'll back off. I just don't want to see you or Andy get hurt."

"I appreciate your concern, Jim, but I'm a big girl. I can take care of myself. And Andy." She saw the hurt in his eyes and reached out to pat his arm. "Please, try to understand."

His lips curved upward, but the smile didn't touch his eyes. "Just promise me you'll be careful."

"I will."

Two hours later, Brittany returned, finding Clint and Andy arguing good-naturedly over who got to feed Ralph.

"Looks like Ralph is getting plenty of attention," she said.

Clint rolled his eyes. "You'd better believe it."

Jim joined them, his expression wry. "I wish all my patients got this much love and attention." He turned to Brittany. "Are you planning on keeping Ralph?"

"I don't think I have much choice." She shifted her gaze back to Andy and his new friend. "I just hope, if someone claims him, he does so before we take Ralph

home. I don't think Andy could bear it if he had to
give Ralph up then.''

The men followed her gaze. She took a moment to
watch them. Both were tall and good-looking. Both
had the build of men accustomed to physical labor.
But there the resemblance stopped.

Jim's blond hair, blue eyes, and open expression
were in sharp contrast to Clint's dark hair and eyes. It
was his eyes, though, that held her attention. They
wore a shuttered look, as though he were afraid of
revealing too much.

Where had she seen that look before? The answer
came quickly. So quickly as to startle her. His eyes
held the same look as hers often did: that of someone
who's been hurt.

He turned to her, jolting her out of her peculiar train
of thought. ''Is something the matter?''

''N . . . no. We'd better be going.''

He gave her a quizzical look. ''If you say so.''

She called Andy, overriding his protests. ''We'll
visit Ralph again. Right now, we've got to get home.''

''Aw, Aunt Brittany.''

Jim laughed. ''Six-year-old boys never change.
That's exactly what I used to say to my mother.''

Brittany smiled. ''And what did she say?''

''Probably the same thing you're going to.''

''We have to go anyway.''

He nodded.

''Can I see Ralph tomorrow, Dr. Jim?'' Andy asked
as he shuffled out.

"Sure thing."

Jim's words stayed with her, casting a shadow over the rest of the day. She felt Clint's gaze upon her several times as she fixed dinner but tried to ignore it.

"Who did the painting?" Clint asked, gesturing to the watercolor of columbines, Colorado's state flower, that hung in the living room. "You?"

"Guilty."

"It's great. Did you do the one in the kitchen with the rainbow peeking out over the barn?"

She nodded. That was her favorite. "I'm really not very good. My painting's strictly a hobby."

"Hey, you aren't maligning my taste, are you?"

She shook her head, smiling in spite of herself. "I'm glad you like it."

"There's something about rainbows . . ."

"I know what you mean." She fingered the tiny rainbow on a silver chain that hung from her neck. "My parents gave me this when I turned twelve. Dad said each of the colors was supposed to represent something. Blue was for honesty."

"It means a lot to you?" Clint asked.

"It did," she said. "A long time ago, it did."

"But you still wear it."

"Some habits are hard to break."

Clint heard the sadness behind the words and wondered at it. It had something to do with the rainbow pendant. But what? And why did Brittany still wear it if it no longer meant anything to her? There was a mystery here. He never could resist a mystery.

He debated staying and talking with her. Then, remembering the hurt, vulnerable look in her eyes that crept in when she thought no one noticed, he vetoed the idea. Besides, he didn't have the right to question her. He'd be here for a week, two at the most, before moving on. Getting involved with his pretty employer was the last thing he wanted to do.

In the barn, Clint inhaled deeply. The combination of fresh hay and clean air was hard to beat. He glanced at his hands and frowned. They'd developed blisters, large, painful ones. He'd been a fool, working without protective gloves. But he'd wanted to *feel* the grain of the wood beneath his hands. He'd pay for that indulgence tomorrow.

Clint Bradley, handyman. He liked it. He liked everything about being here. Most especially, he liked Brittany Howard. She was a contradiction of softness and strength, practicality and whimsy. He also liked Andy. Funny, he'd never given children much thought before.

The house and the fact that it obviously needed care appealed to him. It needed someone like him to put it to rights.

The days fell into a pleasant pattern.

Each morning, Brittany dropped Andy off at the local elementary school, then visited students' homes. She returned home at noon and made lunch, which she and Clint shared. In the afternoon, she taught special education classes.

The house lost its ramshackle air under Clint's repairs. She looked about one day and wondered what they would do when there was nothing else to be fixed. She pushed the thought away.

One evening, they piled into the car, Andy squeezed between Brittany and Clint. She put the car in reverse and groaned when it sputtered. "Not now," she prayed aloud. "Just a little bit longer."

"How long have you had this thing?" Clint asked humorously.

"Not too long. I knew when I bought it that it wouldn't last forever. But I'd hoped it would get me through the year."

He climbed out of the car. "Pop the hood and let me look at it."

She did as instructed and waited for his verdict. Five minutes later, he called, "Try starting it now."

She obeyed and heard the motor hum smoothly.

"You're a miracle worker," she said as he doubled himself over to fit into the cramped interior.

"Not quite. But I do know a thing or two about cars. When we get back, maybe I can take a better look at her."

"Her?"

"Cars are always female. Accounts for their contrariness." He glanced at her. "Present company excepted, of course."

"Of course," she agreed dryly. "But I'm still indebted to you. Anything you can do to keep her running as long as possible will be greatly appreciated."

"I'll do my best, ma'am," he said, sketching an imaginary salute.

"You're a lifesaver."

"I just did a patch job. The whole engine needs an overhaul, but you probably already know that."

"I was afraid of that. Maybe later on."

Ten minutes later, they were slurping double-scoop cones.

Clint dabbed at a spot of chocolate ice cream on Andy's chin with his napkin, then turned his attention to Brittany. "Looks like you and Andy are a lot alike when it comes to eating ice cream." Gently, he wiped a dollop of strawberry from the tip of her nose.

All the while, his attention fixed on her lips, slightly parted, moist with the gooey treat.

She scrubbed at her face with her napkin. "We'd better be going."

"Aw, Aunt Brittany. Do we have to?"

"Your aunt's right," Clint said. "It's getting late."

The trip home was made in relative silence. Only Andy talked, and then only to ask again when their trip might be repeated.

Brittany gave the standard answer. "We'll have to see."

"Okay." He sighed heavily, then brightened. "You didn't say I couldn't ask Clint, did you? Can we go out for ice cream again real soon, Clint?" Andy asked, his childish persistence drawing a smile from both Clint and Brittany.

"As soon as your aunt says so, we'll go again."

She darted a pained look at him. "Now you're making me the heavy."

He grinned. "Sorry about that."

"We can't have ice cream every night, Andy, or it wouldn't be a treat any more, would it?" she asked reasonably.

"I guess not," Andy mumbled, clearly not at all convinced. "But it sure sounds good." He tugged on Clint's sleeve. "What do *you* think?"

"*I* think we better listen to your aunt."

Andy was asleep when they arrived home. Clint lifted him easily and carried him inside. Brittany directed him to the bedroom, where Clint laid the small boy on the single bed.

She touched her lips to Andy's cheek, not bothering to undress him. Better to let him sleep than to risk waking him. *He'd probably want to continue the conversation about a return trip to the ice cream parlor*, she thought with a smile.

Together, she and Clint tiptoed from the room.

"Thanks for going with us tonight," she said. "You didn't have to, but it meant a lot to Andy."

"I wanted to. It's not often I get to be part of a family."

Family. The word still had the power to hurt as she thought of her parents, her sister. They'd been a family once. Before Julie had died. Before . . .

Her smile froze, then disappeared. She turned away from him.

"What's wrong?" Strong hands came to rest on her shoulders.

"Nothing," she said, shrugging off his hands. "Nothing at all."

He turned her to face him. "You're not a very good liar."

"It's really none of your business, is it?" she asked coolly, distancing herself from him physically as well as emotionally.

He dropped his hands. "I guess not," he said, equally distant. "I'll see you in the morning." He walked away without another word.

"Breakfast is at seven."

He gave no acknowledgement that he'd heard her. Brittany replayed every word, relived every gesture between them. Had they meant anything? Or were they merely the product of an overly imaginative mind and a heart too long starved for a bit of attention?

For the last year, she'd denied her womanhood, concentrating all the love she had to give on Andy. Now, her first contact with an attractive man had her acting like a lovesick teenager.

The following morning, she resolved to put Clint Bradley out of her mind. Unfortunately, that was easier said than done, for memories of the precious minutes they had spent together hovered on the edge of her consciousness, destroying all her valiant attempts.

Which was why she should ask him to leave. Before what she was feeling turned to something she couldn't dismiss as fascination or—she grimaced inwardly—frustration.

He was in her thoughts entirely too often. When she drove to her students' homes, he was there. When she graded papers late into the night, thoughts of him interfered with her work.

Admitting defeat, she acknowledged that this man who had found his way into their lives was important to her. Accepting that made her uneasy, for she knew all too well that he would be leaving soon. And when he did, she would be alone again.

She was setting herself up for heartache. Asking him to stay was unthinkable. But asking him to leave would be to cut the heart from her.

For once she pushed aside thoughts of tomorrow. For now, she would accept whatever happiness was offered. Happiness, she knew, could be snatched away without warning.

Chapter Three

The next two weeks were the happiest Brittany had ever known. Never before had she felt so alive, so intensely aware of colors, sounds, and textures. She wanted to sing for the sheer joy of living.

When she allowed herself a rare moment of introspection, she knew the reason for her happiness: Clint. He was becoming more and more important to her. Every day they were together brought fresh delights, special moments to share with one another, such as when they'd found the bird's nest tucked into a rafter of the barn.

"Andy, I found something you might want to see," Clint had said one morning before breakfast, his smile including Brittany.

"What is it?" she had asked.

He'd smiled mysteriously. "Wait and see. It's in the barn."

Curious, she'd tagged along.

"It's up there." He pointed to the rafter above the loft. Andy looked down at his leg braces doubtfully. "I'll help you up the ladder," Clint said.

Ready to object, Brittany looked at Clint and saw the quiet command in his eyes. *Let him do it*, he seemed to say to her. She nodded ever so slightly.

With Clint's help, Andy managed to get up the ladder with an anxious Brittany behind them. With a finger to his lips, Clint pointed to the nest tucked in the joint of the roof rafters.

"Are there babies in it?" Andy whispered.

"Three of 'em. Let me give you a boost and you can see them. Just be careful and don't scare them."

He lifted Andy onto his shoulders.

"They're beautiful. Aunt Brittany, you look too." Clint lowered him to the floor.

"I don't know if I can," she started to demur, when strong hands gripped her waist, and she felt herself being lifted off her feet. "Hey, wait a minute."

Clint held her as easily as he had Andy a moment earlier. "Be quiet and take a peek."

Obediently, she looked inside the nest, where three tiny sparrows stared sightlessly at her. "Oh, I've never seen anything so beautiful."

As he eased her back to the loft floor, she tried to ignore the way her body felt as it slid down the length of his. She resisted the temptation to rest there and reluctantly pulled away.

Clint chuckled. "They're bald and ugly. And you call them beautiful." The teasing light in his eyes belied his derisive words.

"They are," she maintained.

A grin spread across his face. "Anything you say." He took out a handkerchief and wiped a smudge off her nose. "There."

"Hey, I'm hungry," Andy said.

"Seems like I've heard that before," she said, sharing a smile with Clint.

"I think you're right."

The incident was a small one, but it stayed with her, its memory warming her.

Even routine chores took on a new dimension when she was with Clint.

Together, they haunted auctions, antique stores, garage sales. One Saturday morning, Clint cajoled Brittany into attending an estate sale twenty miles away.

"I've got papers to grade," she objected. She didn't really want to spend the morning stuck inside, not when it meant losing a chance to spend the day with Clint. But, still, her conscience insisted that she make at least a token protest.

"So, what are you doing tonight?"

"Tonight? Getting ready for church tomorrow, I guess. What does that have to do with it?"

"What's to stop you from grading the papers tonight?"

"Nothing," she admitted. "I'll have to change first. And get Andy ready."

"He's already set to go." Clint set aside her objections one by one. "And you look fine just the way you are. More than fine," he added.

His tone, more than the words, caused hot color to smudge her cheeks. "Let me brush my hair, and I'll be ready," she promised, more to give herself something to do than because her hair really needed anything. His words had flustered her, causing unwarranted feelings to thrust through her normal composure.

She turned away, fishing for a brush from her purse. Self-consciously, she drew it through her hair, trying to restore some order to the unruly curls that defied her attempts to control them.

Clint gently took the brush from her. "You don't need to do anything. You always look wonderful. To me."

His arms encircled her waist, and she allowed herself the luxury of leaning against him.

"You smell so good," he said, tightening his arms around her.

It felt good, she acknowledged silently. Secure in his arms, she could almost believe they belonged together. It felt so natural, so right. Could it possibly last more than a few days, a few weeks? Did he feel it too?

Her feelings threatened to explode. She pulled away.

"What about lunch? Are you expecting us to set forth on this expedition without food?"

"All taken care of," he said easily. He understood her need to put some distance between them. Yet he couldn't help being disappointed. He didn't let it show in his voice. "Andy and I packed a picnic basket while a certain sleepyhead was still in bed."

"Look." Andy held out the heavy basket for her inspection.

She took a quick peek. "Where'd all this come from?"

Clint looked a little sheepish. "We made a quick trip to the deli. Hope you don't mind?"

She tried to look stern but failed miserably. "How could I?" She ruffled Andy's hair. "Were you in on this too?"

"Sure was," he said proudly.

The confident tone of his voice, the bright anticipation shining in his eyes, caused her to catch her breath. She owed Clint a lot. He was good for Andy. Good for them both. In more ways than one.

Only one incident marred the developing relationship between them. Their evenings had assumed a comfortable pattern where Brittany graded papers while Clint read the newspaper.

"Mind if I ask you something?" he asked one evening when she'd finished the last of the "What I Did on My Summer Vacation" essays.

She shook her head, knowing what was coming.

"How did you . . ."

"How did I end up with Andy?"

He nodded.

"My sister, Julie, and her husband were killed in an accident. Andy survived, but his legs were badly damaged."

"But why you? Wasn't there someone else? Another sister or brother?"

She smiled. "I'm twenty-six." Her smile dimmed. "There's no one else. Julie and I are . . . were . . . the only children. My parents had Andy for a while, but they're both in their sixties."

"Where do your folks live?"

"Colorado Springs."

"I guess you see them pretty often."

She busied herself with scraping dishes. "No, we don't," she said shortly, hoping he'd drop the subject. He refused to take the hint.

"Why not?"

"We had a disagreement about something."

"Must have been a pretty big something."

"It was."

He waited, clearly not about to let her off the hook.

"I was living out of state when Julie and Dave were killed. I came as soon as I heard. When I arrived, I learned my parents hadn't told Andy that his parents were dead. They said Julie and Dave were on a trip and wouldn't be back for a long time. I tried to keep up the pretense. And I did, for a while. But I couldn't live a lie. So, I told Andy the truth." A spasm of pain

crossed her face as she remembered the scene that
followed. "My parents were livid."

"What happened?"

"They told me I'd probably caused Andy to have a
setback, one he might never rally from."

"Did it?"

"The doctors didn't think so. They thought all along
Andy should know the truth."

"But your parents didn't see it that way," he said.

"You could say that."

She twisted a strand of hair. For a while, it appeared
her parents had been right. Andy had refused to talk,
refused to eat, until the nurses were forced to feed him
intravenously. Then he'd rallied. But it hadn't made a
difference to her parents. Brittany had defied them.
She, in turn, felt they'd betrayed Andy and her with
their lies.

"It hurt for a while, but that's better than having
him wait for his parents who aren't ever going to come
back."

She waited for his nod, the confirmation that she'd
done the right thing. It didn't come. His next words
surprised her.

"You haven't seen your parents since then?"

"No. Their lies cost too much. I wasn't willing to
pay that price." When she realized he wasn't going to
agree with her, she felt her defenses shift into place.

"Have you looked at it from their side?" he asked.
"Sure, your parents were wrong, asking you to lie to
Andy. But did you ever think that they were hurting

too? They'd just lost a daughter. They probably wanted to spare him that kind of heartache.''

''And I'd lost a sister.'' Her voice turned husky with pain that was still raw. ''I thought you'd understand.''

''I do.''

''Do I hear a but in there somewhere?''

''Somewhere along the line you need to forgive your parents for not being perfect. They were just people trying to do the best they could under difficult circumstances.''

His censure hurt. ''I'd better turn in. It's been a long day.''

She lay awake far into the night, unable to forget the conversation. Clint was wrong. Just as her parents had been wrong. Lying was never justified. Even to spare someone pain. Why couldn't he understand that?

She slipped the rainbow pendant from beneath her gown, tracing its outlines. Blue was for honesty, her father had said. Why had he let her down?

Brittany fingered the rainbow pendant as she cradled the phone under her chin. Men from the phone company had come only that morning to install it.

''Yes, Mrs. Johnson, I'll ask him about it.'' She hung up the phone, frowning.

''Andy, that was your teacher. She said you had a note that you were supposed to give me yesterday. Is that right?''

Clearly unhappy, he nodded.

''Where is it?''

"I lost it," he said in a small voice.

"You're sure?"

"Yes." He opened his back pack. "See? It's not here."

"What did it say?"

"I don't remember."

"Then you wouldn't know how it wound up in the trash can in your classroom?" she asked. "Mrs. Johnson told me she found it there."

"No . . ." His lip trembled. "I threw it away. I didn't want you to know I wasn't doing well in spelling."

"There's nothing wrong with having a hard time in spelling. But lying is never right," Brittany said, hugging him to her. "You never have to be afraid to tell me anything, Andy. Just don't lie to me. Nothing could be so bad that you have to lie about it. Okay?"

"Okay."

Planing the screen door, Clint listened to the exchange with a mix of admiration and growing uneasiness. He knew how Brittany felt about dishonesty. She'd made it plain enough. How was he going to explain the lies he'd told her, if only by omission?

He hadn't really lied, he defended himself silently. After all, Brittany was the one who told him that he was an out-of-work handyman. He just hadn't bothered to correct it.

He considered doing it now, but rejected the idea. She wasn't likely to understand, and he was strangely loathe to leave this job. For the first time in years, he was happy. He spent his days working with his hands, restoring and repairing the old house. By the end of the day, he was bone tired but satisfied.

It'd be time to move along soon enough. With luck, Brittany would never need know the truth. They'd both benefited from the arrangement. But he didn't want to leave yet. Soon, he told himself, but not yet.

He found himself looking forward to Saturday. He and Brittany planned to attend an estate auction. When she learned he'd never gone to one, she scanned the paper and circled an ad in the classifieds. "We'll go this Saturday. We're sure to find lots of bargains."

The idea appealed to Clint. Unbidden, a picture of his ex-fiancée surfaced. When had Sherry ever considered bargain hunting? The answer was easy. Never.

But then Brittany was nothing like Sherry. She was like no one he'd ever known before.

Clint dropped the screwdriver he'd been using to tighten a bolt as the truth hit him. He'd been lying to himself. He had no intention of leaving. Ever. Brittany and Andy were fast becoming important to him. Only one thing stood between them.

The truth.

The day was brushed with magic.

A golden haze gilded the landscape of sun-cured prairie grasses with the shimmering heat of early September. Prairie dogs peered from their burrows, barked madly, then scrambled deep into their underground homes. A crow cawed, establishing his domain. The small lakes that dotted the area reflected the brilliance of the sky. Meticulously planted rows of corn stood like soldiers filed in queue.

And, through it all, was Clint.

He had only to reach out his hand to touch her own, and she trembled with an inner pleasure so intense it frightened her. It made no sense. No sense at all. Yet it was there.

She ignored the niggling voice that told her it wouldn't last.

With Andy squeezed in between them in the front seat, there was little opportunity for privacy, but it made no difference. His presence only heightened Brittany's joy. Ralph, who'd insisted on accompanying them, snored loudly in the back seat.

She smiled as she remembered Ralph's first night at their home. She'd made a bed for him in the kitchen and firmly led him there with the command to "stay."

He had looked at her with mournful brown eyes. Ten minutes later, he'd appeared at the foot of Andy's bed, establishing a spot for himself by burrowing in the covers.

Brittany had tried scolding, coaxing, and pleading, to no avail. Finally, she'd given in. Ralph now slept with Andy permanently. Nothing short of an earthquake could move him.

Ralph fit into their lives with the ease of someone who knows his rightful place. His leg healed completely, and he romped happily through the house. Somehow, though, he must have sensed his master's disability for, after a few days, he slowed his pace to match Andy's awkward one.

She felt Clint's gaze upon her and smiled.

"Daydreaming?" he asked.

"I was just thinking how happy I am."

The warm glow in her eyes, the soft smile on her lips, were almost more than he could bear. He wanted to take her in his arms and kiss her until they were both breathless. Instead, he said only, "I'm glad."

Brittany smiled sunnily at him. She wanted to reach out and capture the happiness that beckoned to her. For so long, it had been denied her. Was it wrong to want to seize this brief moment of joy?

For now, for this moment in time, her world was complete.

For now.

"What are we looking for today?" Deliberately, she interrupted her own reverie, afraid of where her thoughts were leading.

"Anything we want. That's half the fun. Finding the unexpected. Speaking of the unexpected . . . " He glanced at the sleeping Ralph.

She grinned. "I couldn't leave him. He cried when I started to tie him up."

"He cried?" Clint gave her a skeptical look.

"Like a baby."

He tweaked her nose. "You spoil him. That's all right," he said when she started to defend herself. "I love you for it."

I love you. Did he mean it? Not in the way you want

him to, she told herself. Determinedly, she pushed aside worries about the future and concentrated on today.

"I hope we find a football," Andy said, disturbing her self-absorption.

"We'll make it our first order of business," Clint said, "before we look for anything else."

They didn't find the football. But it didn't matter.

Unexpected treasures, tucked away in dark corners of the old homestead, created a furor among eager bargain hunters. Clint and Brittany, Andy and Ralph were no exception.

"Clint," she called. "Look, a butter churn."

"And what will you do with it?"

She threw him an exasperated glance. "I'll refinish it and use it, of course. I've always wanted to try making my own butter." She examined it more closely. The lid, complete with handle, had been formed from a solid piece of walnut, the base from oak.

In the end, they purchased the churn, an antique quilt in the double wedding ring pattern that needed only a new binding, and several pieces of Depression glass.

"Look how the light shimmers through this." She held out a butter press, the bottom engraved with a cloverleaf imprint, for Clint's inspection. "Isn't it beautiful?"

"Beautiful."

She smiled up at him, to find his eyes on her rather than the delicately tinted pink glass.

"I meant the butter dish," she said, her breath catching slightly at the expression in his eyes.

"I think we've each found what we wanted."

There was no mistaking his meaning, and she savored the delicious warmth that spread throughout her body.

"Can we eat now?" Andy's plaintive tone jarred her out of the pleasurable track her thoughts had been following.

Clint laughed. "First things first. And food is definitely in order."

They found a grassy spot shaded by an ancient tree. There, they spread out the old blanket he had stashed in the back of the car.

Brittany began laying out their lunch. "It looks like there's enough here for an army. Several armies," she said, examining the contents of the basket more thoroughly and frowning. "How did you—"

"I, uh, had a bit of money saved up and decided to splurge," Clint said. "With free room and board, I don't have much to spend it on."

"I don't know. It seems like an awful lot."

"We men need a lot to keep us going, don't we?" he interrupted, laying an arm about Andy's shoulders.

Andy nodded. "You bet."

They bought cups of lemonade from a stand set up by two enterprising boys. Brittany and Clint munched on apples and spread the crusty bread with tangy mustard. Andy impatiently wolfed down one sandwich before demanding dessert.

Laughingly, she agreed. "Just this once."

"What's a picnic for, anyway, if not to eat too much and then feel sick?" Clint asked.

Together they polished off the spice cake, with Brittany and Clint arguing over who should get the last piece.

Ralph settled the argument by licking the piece, then turned injured eyes on Clint as Clint swatted him.

"That beast is spoiled rotten."

Andy buried his head in Ralph's shaggy fur. "He was just hungry, weren't you, boy?"

Clint tried to look stern and failed.

Brittany grinned. "You're as bad as the rest of us. I saw you sneaking bites of your sandwich to him."

"Guilty as charged."

"You're a softie." Replete, she lay back on the blanket. "I'm stuffed. I don't think I'll ever eat again."

"Then I guess you won't want to stop for a milk shake on the way home."

"Chocolate?"

"What else?"

"Please, Aunt Brittany. Can we? I'm starved."

Brittany and Clint burst out laughing. Bewildered, Andy looked from one to the other.

"Just what have you been doing for the last half hour?" she asked.

"Eating. So?"

"So, why are you hungry now?" Clint asked the obvious.

"I used up a lot of energy eating."

Clint shook his head at the irrefutable logic of a six-year-old. "He's got me there." He began gathering up the remains of their picnic. "Want to look around anymore?"

About to shake her head no, she changed her mind. "Would you mind if I poked through one more barrel?"

"Aw—" Andy protested.

"Come on, Andy," Clint said easily. "We've got all day. Dairy Queen will still be there."

"Okay. But don't be too long, will you?"

"Just a few minutes," Brittany promised.

Together, they returned to the barn, and she found the barrel she'd noticed earlier. "Mind if I go through this?" she asked one of the owners.

"Nope. Don't rightly know what's in there. Just help yourself."

She began pulling out old blankets, a broken lantern, and a plastic bag full of quilt scraps. "Doesn't look like there's any treasure here." A glint of color caught her eye. Quickly, she dug deeper and found the object. "Clint, look." She held up a crystal mobile, catching all the colors of the rainbow.

She touched each crystal in awe. "Look."

"Beautiful," he murmured, his eyes resting on her. "I've never seen one like it. May I?" He held out his hand.

Reverently, she handed it to him.

He turned to the old man. "How much for this?"

The man scratched his chin. "Don't rightly know. Make an offer, and I'll let you know if it's enough."

Clint grinned. "Sounds fair. Fifteen dollars all right?"

"Yep."

As he reached into his pocket, Brittany placed a hand on his. "I'll pay for it." He looked like he wanted to protest, but then shrugged.

The transaction made, Brittany, Clint, and Andy left the barn. "I can't let you pay for everything," she said quietly as they walked to the car.

"I wanted it to be a gift."

"This day has been gift enough," she said, her voice quiet but firm. "I'll always remember it."

"So will I."

Andy scuffled ahead of them. "Come on, Clint. You promised we'd stop for milk shakes, and I'm hungry." His long-suffering look reminded Brittany that they'd been in the barn far longer than she'd planned.

Clint hefted Andy onto his shoulders. "Race you to the car," he called to Brittany.

"You're on."

Andy wrapped his arms around Clint's neck as they galloped to the car, with Ralph running circles around them.

Breathless, Brittany reached the car seconds later.

Settled in between them in the front seat, Andy promptly fell asleep.

Dusk had crept quietly into evening, and the sky was alive with an artist's palette of colors. Bold strokes of peach vied with vivid purple for dominance. Farther on the horizon, a dazzling rose served as a stage for the jagged peaks of the Rockies.

Awed by nature's colors that an artist would kill for, she sucked in her breath. "I never get tired of this land. It's never the same but always the same."

Clint pressed her hand. "I know what you mean."

She glanced down at Andy. "Looks like Andy wasn't as hungry as he thought." Gently, she brushed a stray strand of hair from his forehead.

"What if we stop at a store and pick up some ice cream to have later on at home?"

"You always know what to do." Instinctively, she scooted closer to him, a contented smile on her lips.

Clint inhaled deeply. Her hair smelled of the fruity shampoo she favored and reminded him of a freshly picked peach. It was crazy, this wild desire to kiss her, to taste the soft lips that curved up at him so delectably.

He returned the smile and wished he'd been who he pretended to be: an ordinary laborer, down on his luck. Then, maybe then, they would have stood a chance together.

When he kissed her good night, he could barely restrain himself from telling her how he felt.

The nights in the barn grew increasingly long. Clint tried reading, propping up a lantern. Its flickering light cast soft shadows over the barn, causing his mind to wander. The books fell to the floor after only a few pages.

He counted sheep. He did more push-ups than he'd ever done in the Marines.

One afternoon, after they'd finished the lunch dishes and Andy was still at school, Clint led Brittany to the swing on the front porch.

"We have to talk." He hesitated. "I've taken a room in town."

She looked up at him with bewildered eyes. "Why?"

"This is a small town. People talk. I don't want them talking about you."

"But we haven't . . . I mean . . . "

He put a finger to her lips. "I know. But that doesn't change human nature. I've found a room in the basement of a house. It's not much, but it suits my needs. Otherwise, nothing's changed. I'll still be here for breakfast and work through dinner. If that's all right with you?"

"Of course."

"There's something else I want to tell—"

"I'm home." Andy dragged his legs up the porch steps.

Clint sighed, his regret sharply mixed with relief that he hadn't had to make his confession yet.

Awkwardly, Andy shuffled across the porch. "Aunt Brittany, Clint, I got to be scorekeeper in soccer today at recess. Coach said he needed someone to turn over the numbers."

Clint stood and swung the little boy off his feet.

"That's great." Still holding Andy, he pulled Brittany up to join them in a bear hug.

"This deserves a celebration," she said. "How about cake for dessert tonight?"

"Chocolate cake with chocolate ice cream?" Andy asked.

"Chocolate cake *and* chocolate ice cream?"

"I want a double scoop."

Clint smiled over the small blond head at Brittany. "Sounds like we're in for a treat tonight." Gently, he lowered Andy to the floor.

"And a lot of calories," Brittany smiled. "I intend to enjoy every one of them."

"Hey." Andy tugged at her hand. "I'm hungry."

"Don't tell me. You want a snack to tide you over until dinner."

He nodded. "Peanut butter and jelly and bologna."

"If you keep playing soccer and eating like this, we're going to have to move closer to a grocery store."

He grinned. "That'd be neat. I could have all the candy and cookies and ice cream that I want if we owned a grocery store."

"We'd better know a good dentist then," she said.

"Aw, Aunt Brittany."

Brittany ruffled his hair. "That's what aunts are for."

"I guess so."

Clint watched the interchange with amusement, his eyes softening as he took in the love that shone through the bantering. He wanted to be part of that love. He wanted to be a permanent part of it.

Yet he was here under false pretenses and still hadn't told her the truth. How could he even begin to put it into words?

The answer came swiftly. He couldn't. At least, not yet.

He had to buy time, he argued with himself. Time to let his relationship with Brittany deepen. Time to let her trust him just a little more. Time, he admitted to himself, to muster up as much courage as he possibly could to face the biggest challenge of his life.

The stakes riding on it were the highest he'd ever played for. If he won, the world was his. If he lost—

If he lost, nothing else mattered.

For three years, he had fought in the jungles of Vietnam. Fear had become a way of life. He had lived with it, slept in spite of it, and tasted it until it was as much a part of him as breathing. Yet he'd gladly face another grueling crawl through enemy territory rather than tell Brittany the truth. A self-loathing tainted his mouth with a bitter tang as he thought of how he'd worked his way into her life. Now he needed every bit of nerve he possessed just to face her.

"Clint, did you want to tell me something?" Brittany asked.

"It doesn't matter. It'll keep."

"But—"

"I said it will keep." His voice sharper than he intended, he manufactured a smile. "I've already for-

gotten it, so it must not have been very important.''
The lie cankered inside of him. Sooner or later he
would have to tell her.

Brittany touched his arm. ''If you're in trouble, I
want to help.''

*Love me and let me be a part of your life. Love me
enough not to hate me when you learn that I've been
lying to you from the beginning.*

''It's nothing. Now, what say we start that cake you
promised?'' His eyes met her troubled gaze. He knew
she was puzzled, but he was powerless to tell her what
she needed to hear.

Chapter Four

A school holiday gave Brittany a day off, which she planned to spend wallpapering her bedroom. Soon Clint and Andy were helping her.

"You're going to put flowers on your wall?" Andy asked in disgust as she unrolled the paper.

She nodded, feeling like she'd just committed an unpardonable offense. "What's wrong with flowers?"

"Girls like them," Andy said, in the tone of one explaining the obvious.

"In case you haven't noticed, I'm a girl."

"You're Aunt Brittany," Andy corrected, rolling his eyes.

Clint wrapped his arms around her waist. "*I* know you're a girl," he whispered, his lips whispering a kiss to the sensitive spot behind her ear. "You're also very much a woman."

"Hey, we gonna do this or not?" Andy asked.

Guiltily, Brittany stepped away from Clint. "Who wants to paste and who wants to trim?"

"I'll paste," Andy volunteered.

She cut the strips of wallpaper while Andy brushed paste onto them. "Now, all we have to do is get this to the wall without ripping it."

"Reporting for duty, ma'am," Clint said, giving his smartest salute.

Together, they picked up a strip and started toward the nearest wall.

Ralph bolted into the room. He took one look at the carefully cut strips and pounced on top of them.

"Oh, no!" Brittany shouted.

Clint wrestled Ralph away, but not before the dog had managed to leave muddy paw prints across the wallpaper and knocked over the bucket of paste.

"Bad dog," she scolded.

"I'm taking him outside and chaining him to the clothesline," Clint announced.

"He didn't mean to be bad," Andy defended his friend. "He was just feeling left out."

"That's too bad, because he's out of here as of now." Clint half pushed, half dragged Ralph from the room. Mournful woofs could be heard from the other side of the door.

"Come on, Andy, let's get this mess cleaned up,"

she said. Together, they threw away the wasted strips
and mopped up the spilled paste.

Just as they were finishing, Clint returned.

"Did you chain him up?" she asked.

He avoided her gaze. "Well, uh, I decided maybe
he'd learned his lesson. He's lying down on the porch
right now. I think he's tired."

She clamped a hand over her mouth but couldn't
stop the explosion of laughter that erupted.

"I gave him a lecture," Clint said. "I don't think
he'll try anything like that again."

Brittany put her arms around his neck. "You're a
pushover."

He returned the hug. "If this is the reward I get,
maybe I'll try being a pushover more often."

Aware that Andy was watching them, she pulled
away. Only then did she notice the dirty streaks across
Clint's shirt.

"Uh-oh. It looks like Ralph tried to give you a hug
too."

He looked down at his shirt. "Ugh. I hate to think
where he's been." He reached for a towel to wipe
away the smudges but only succeeded in smearing them
further.

"I think it's a lost cause," she said.

"It doesn't look so bad," Andy said. "I like brown
shirts."

"I do too, except when they're supposed to be
white," Clint said. "Oh, well, it's all in a good cause.

Let's get back to work before Ralph forgets the lesson he's supposed to have learned.''

Two hours later, they stepped back to admire their work.

"If I do say so myself, it looks pretty good," Brittany said. "Just one more thing." She took the double wedding ring quilt from its protective wrapping and spread it on the bed. "There."

"Beautiful," Clint said as his gaze rested on her.

"Beautiful," she agreed.

"What's so great about an old quilt?" Andy demanded.

With a groan, Clint collapsed onto the floor, dragging a giggling Andy with him. "We men worked up an appetite. If we don't get lunch soon, I won't be responsible for the consequences."

"Yeah, us men are hungry," Andy seconded.

At that moment, Ralph wandered into the room, took in the situation, and hurtled toward them. Enthusiastically, he licked Clint's face with a rough pink tongue.

"Enough already." Clint pushed him away. "So much for Ralph learning a lesson."

"And he had such a good teacher," Brittany murmured.

Clint gave her a suspicious look. "What's that supposed to mean?"

"Nothing."

He helped Andy up. "What about going out for lunch?"

"Whoopee," Andy shouted.

"Maybe we'd better—"

"After all the work we put in, we deserve it," Clint said, overriding Brittany's objections.

Andy put his hands on his hips. "Yeah."

In the end, they compromised. Andy and Clint went to buy take-out chicken while Brittany cleaned up the mess.

Licking her fingers an hour later, she sighed appreciatively. "I have to admit this was a good idea. I really didn't feel like cooking."

Clint grinned. "I like a woman who recognizes a good plan when she hears one."

"Do you like Aunt Brittany, Clint?" Andy asked.

The innocent question startled him. "I like her very much," he said at last.

Andy turned his attention on Brittany. "Do you like Clint?"

She nodded cautiously, certain he was leading up to something embarrassing.

"Then why don't you get married?"

She looked to Clint for help. A grin split his face in half.

"Big help you are." She turned to face Andy. "Why all this talk about marriage?"

"Johnny Moore's big sister is getting married because she's in love."

"Oh."

"If you and Clint are in love too . . . "

She knew she was blushing, but couldn't help it. "It's not that simple."

"Why not?"

"Yeah, why not?" Clint echoed the question.

Brittany glared at him while she tried to formulate an answer that a six-year-old could understand. "You said Johnny's sister is in love. Clint and I are only in like."

Andy screwed up his face in thought. "In like? Is that sort of like being in love, only not so much?"

"That's right." She drew a relieved breath.

"So after you're in like, then will you be in love? That's the way it happened with Johnny Moore's sister."

She looked at him in exasperation. "We don't know yet."

"Oh."

"Don't we?" Clint murmured.

"No, we don't," she snapped. She looked at Andy, who was yawning widely. She frowned when she saw him absently rub his leg. "I know someone who needs a nap."

"Not me."

Another yawn escaped, and both Clint and Brittany laughed.

"Come on," she coaxed. "You've worked hard. Even grown-ups take naps sometimes."

Andy looked to Clint for confirmation. "Really?"

"Really."

"Well, maybe just a little one."

"Would you like a piggyback ride into bed?"

"Naw, that's for babies."

"I know some mighty big babies then. My dad used to give me piggyback rides when I was way bigger than you." Clint bit back a grin as Andy thought it over.

"All right."

Clint knelt down while Andy climbed on his back. He returned ten minutes later. "I stayed till he fell asleep." He gave her a curious look. "Don't you think he's a little old for naps?"

"If he gets too tired, his legs begin hurting. I could tell when he started rubbing his thigh."

He touched her cheek. "I'm sorry. I didn't mean to criticize."

"It's all right." She studied her nails. "I'm the one who ought to apologize."

He looked surprised. "What for?"

"Andy's matchmaking. He didn't know what he was saying."

"I think he knew exactly what he was saying."

"He's only six—"

"Hey, it's okay. I only wish I could convince his aunt."

He didn't mean it.

"What else is on the agenda today, boss lady?" he asked, his question bringing them back to safe ground.

She smiled, grateful for the change of subject. "I thought of painting the fence. I've been wanting to do that ever since Andy and I moved here."

"You're a real slave driver, aren't you?"

"If you'd rather not—"

He looked out the window at the picket fence, its once white color now a dingy gray. "There's something about a white picket fence," he said, more to himself than to her.

But she heard the wistfulness behind the words. "There is, isn't there? Somehow, it spells home to me. I guess that's the main reason I picked this place." She gave a wry smile. "That, and the price was right."

"Yeah." He knew what she meant about the fence. That was her symbol. He had his own.

It had been more than thirty years ago. But the feelings were as powerful as though it were yesterday.

He had come home from school. The door to the small tract house was open. He'd rushed in. The aroma of chocolate cake wafted out to tantalize his nostrils. "Mom, I'm home!"

But it wasn't his mother who greeted him. It was the neighbor. His mother had been taken to the hospital, two hours before. An embolism, lodged in her leg, had traveled to her heart. The cake she'd been baking now rested on the counter, cooling. It had been chocolate, his favorite.

Chocolate cake. A child's memory. Perhaps that was why he had refused to eat it for years, until a couple of nights ago with Brittany and Andy.

Brittany brushed his cheek, her hand soft and warm. "What is it?" she asked.

Clint jerked away from it and pretended not to notice the hurt that crossed her face. With an effort, he brought himself back to the present. "Do you have any paint?"

"Just so happens I do. I bought it with some mad money."

"The best kind to have."

"It is, isn't it? Then you don't have to account for it. To anybody. No even to yourself."

Though she spoke lightly, he recognized the significance of her words. In the last year, she hadn't had much mad money, he guessed.

"You have here a ready and willing slave, so point me to it."

Two hours later, they looked at the now gleaming white fence. It reflected a bright shaft of sunlight and actually made the scrubby yard appear almost green.

Brittany handed him a glass of lemonade.

Wiping his forehead with the back of his hand, he accepted the drink with thanks. He had long since stripped off his shirt, and his chest and shoulders, bronzed by the sun, glistened under a fine sheen of sweat.

She couldn't help but notice his hard musculature, and she flushed as she realized that his eyes had followed the direction of her gaze.

Clint picked up his shirt. "I could use a shower. All right if I use the one in the house?"

"Why wait?" She turned the hose on him, soaking his hair and clothes. She kept it aimed at him until he wrestled it away from her.

"Your turn now, sweetheart."

She ducked to avoid the spray of cold water, but not fast enough to elude him. He grabbed her around the waist and held the hose directly over her head. Giggling, she tried to wrench free, but only succeeded in falling against him.

When they were both soaked, he threw the hose down and pulled her to him. The laughter was gone from his eyes. Head lowered, he found his goal as his lips settled upon hers.

She tilted her head back, her mouth eager for his. Infinitely slow, he grazed her lips with his own, lightly at first, then more deeply as the kiss intensified. A promise given and received.

A soft moan trembled from her lips. She reveled in his strength, which was tempered by a sweet gentleness.

"Brittany, you make me feel things I didn't even know existed."

I know, she responded silently.

The picture shifted suddenly, and they were a family: Clint, Andy, and herself, with the promise of more children to come. She'd always wanted a big family.

Clint fingered the wet curls framing her face and gently twined one around his finger.

"You're shivering."

"I'd better go change," she said.

"I'll clean up out here."

She started toward the house, then paused. "Don't you want to use the shower?"

"No, thanks. I changed my mind."

She took an uncertain step forward. He watched her retreating back, a sigh escaping his lips.

Inside, Brittany pulled off her wet clothes, shuddered violently, and wished that it were only from cold. Goosebumps puckered her flesh, and she turned on the shower, hoping its heat would quiet her quivering limbs.

As hot water sluiced over her, she relived those moments with Clint, replaying each in her mind.

You're making too much of a simple kiss.

It wasn't simple at all.

A kiss is a kiss.

Not when it feels as if your bones are melting and your mind starts imagining all sorts of impossible things.

He's probably forgotten all about it.

No. He'd been affected as she had been.

The hot water had gradually turned tepid and now was decidedly cool. She stepped out of the shower, wrapped herself in a towel, and stared at her reflection in the mirror.

She didn't look any different. Then why did she feel as though her feelings were written across her face, plain for all to see?

Quickly, she toweled off, then dug through her drawers for fresh underwear. She pulled on jeans and a plaid shirt. "Aunt Brittany! Where are you?"

"In here." She stepped out of the room to find Andy standing in the doorway.

He gave her a reproachful look. "How come you and Clint painted the fence without me?"

Brittany crossed the room to kneel down in front of him. "I'm sorry, Andy. You were still asleep. I didn't think you'd mind."

"I wanted to help." His lower lip jutted out.

"There'll be lots more things to paint around here. Clint thinks the whole house will need a new coat pretty soon."

Andy's eyes brightened. "Can I help?"

"You bet. Now, you'd better wash up for dinner. Okay?"

"Okay." He scuffled away.

Brittany watched his awkward gait. The braces didn't slow him down too much—now. But the doctors had warned that as he grew, his legs would grow weaker, unable to support the increased weight. An operation might be possible, they said, when he was a bit older. That had been a year ago.

There had been so many operations and hospital stays in the last two years. She hated to subject him to another. But if it could help . . .

Thoughtfully, she walked into the kitchen. She sat down at the table and yanked a brush through her hair.

"Hey, that's no way to do it." A gentle hand halted the brush.

Brittany turned and found Clint gazing at her quizzically.

"Something the matter?" he asked.

"I was just thinking."

His eyes searched her face. "From the way you were wielding that hair brush, I hope I wasn't the subject."

"I was thinking about Andy. About the future."

"There aren't any easy answers, are there?"

She shook her head. "No. I wish there were. Just this once."

He placed large hands on her shoulders. "I'm here. If you want to talk about it. Okay?"

"Thanks." She shook off her anxiety. "What would you say to dinner?"

"I'd say great. I'm starved."

"Poor boy," she crooned. "Maybe some food will cheer you up."

The rest of the evening was sprinkled with stardust because they were together. By unspoken consent, neither Clint nor Brittany referred to the kiss. She hugged it to her, storing it away in that secret place in her heart where precious memories may be taken out to pause and linger over.

She refused to believe that was all she might have of him.

Chapter Five

Brittany bit her lip in exasperation. "Mr. Tolley, if you'd only give me a chance—give Robbie a chance— we might surprise you. Why won't you let him go to school? He wants to, more than he lets on."

"Why should he go to school? Don't you come here each week? Ain't he getting enough schoolin' without going there where the kids are going to laugh at him?" Hard, calloused hands gripped the handle of the shovel more tightly, the knuckles whitening under the pressure.

"It won't be like that," she promised, understanding his fear. "Robbie . . . " She groped for the right words. "Robbie is a bright boy; he's quick and eager to learn. He has a learning disability. Some of the most brilliant men and women of this century have had learning

71

disabilities. Look at Winston Churchill and Albert Einstein. It didn't stop them, and it won't stop Robbie. But we have to give him the opportunity to be like other little boys his age. Give him this chance, Mr. Tolley. Please.''

A work-roughened hand brushed tiredly across his eyes. "I don't know, Miss Howard," he said at last. "The last school we sent him to, the kids there kept after him with their teasing and name-calling till he just quit going. I don't want that happening again. I couldn't stand seeing him like that." Tears pooled in the corners of his eyes.

Touched by the unexpected emotion from this hard-working man, Brittany said gently, "It won't, Mr. Tolley. Stansberry Elementary School has programs designed for children with special needs. Robbie will have the chance to learn, and what's more important, he'll be with other kids while he's doing it. Right now, that's more important than anything else.''

Tired eyes, fanned with lines etched by long hours in the sun, regarded her with new respect. "You really care about my Robbie, don't you?"

She smiled. "Yes, I do. I want what's best for him, just like you do.''

"And you believe that this will be best—sending him to this school?" His eyes begged her to tell him the truth.

"I wouldn't be here if I didn't.''

"Then we'll give it a try.''

"Thank you, Mr. Tolley. You won't regret it." She crossed her fingers that she could keep her promise.

"He was so angry," she told Clint later that evening. "At first, I thought it was directed at me. Then, I realized it was because he loved his son so much. He didn't want Robbie to be hurt again."

"But you did it," he said warmly. "You convinced him that letting Robbie go to school with other kids was the right thing to do."

Her cheeks reddened under his praise, and she felt a warmth spread throughout her that had nothing to do with the lingering heat of the day.

"It wasn't me," she said. "It was Mr. Tolley himself. He truly wants what's best for his son. All I did was point out a few things to him. It can't have been easy for him, raising a boy on his own." At the question in Clint's eyes, she explained, "Robbie told me his mother left them a few years back. I don't know, of course, but I'm guessing she couldn't cope with having a child with special needs."

"That's rough. On the boy and his dad."

"I know," she said feelingly. "Raising a child on your own is never easy, especially when the child has special needs."

"Is something wrong?" she asked when several minutes had elapsed and he had said nothing. *Had she bored him with her news about Robbie and his dad?*

"No, nothing's wrong. I was just thinking . . ." He didn't complete the sentence, but drew her close.

She went willingly. His arms closed about her, and

she reveled in their gentleness. He had shown her that a man could be strong yet tender. Just by being himself, he had let her glimpse the promise of what could be between a man and a woman.

Had he also shown her how to love?

She pushed the thought away. It was too soon to be thinking about love. Clint cared about her. That was enough for now.

"What did you do before you came here?" she asked.

Clint hesitated. *Now was his chance. Tell her.*

He watched as her fingers twisted the rainbow pendant. And he knew he couldn't tell her. She hadn't been able to forgive her own parents for their dishonesty. How did he expect her to forgive him?

"I'm just someone who was tired of the rat race of the city. Someday I'll have to go back. But not yet." *Never, if it means leaving you.*

"I'm glad. That you don't have to go back yet, I mean."

"Brittany, you know how I feel. I want—"

She touched her fingers to his lips. "Don't. Not yet."

"Is it me?"

"No, it's me. I'm not ready. I'm not sure I ever will be. I can't ask you or any man to take on a ready-made family. Especially one with the extra challenges we have. I had to make a choice once—between Andy and the man I thought I loved. I chose Andy."

"The guy was a jerk," Clint said. "If he couldn't accept Andy, you're better off without him."

"He was selfish, sure. But so was I. I expected too much of him."

"You didn't expect too much. Any man, any real man, would be proud to have Andy for a son."

She traced the line of his jaw. "I know I've asked for time before. And now I'm asking again."

He took her hands in his own. "You're still afraid, aren't you? Of trusting again."

He read the answer in her eyes.

"Hey, what's going on in here?" Andy's sleepy voice startled them out of their private world.

"Not a thing, pal," Clint said easily. He casually removed his arm from around Brittany's shoulders and held out a welcoming hand.

Andy shuffled over to join them. "Are you and Aunt Brittany having secrets? I heard you talking."

Clint recognized the accusing tone and sought to reassure the little boy. "No, Andy, we aren't. But sometimes we like to talk with each other. Just like you and I talk together. Right?"

"I guess so."

He hoisted Andy onto his shoulders. "Ready for a piggyback ride back to bed?"

"You bet." Andy tightened his arms around Clint's neck and grinned down at Brittany.

When Clint emerged from the bedroom a few minutes later, he rubbed a hand across his brow with an exaggerated sigh.

"That boy's got the energy of six six-year-olds."

"*You're* telling *me?*"

"Guess you already knew that, huh?"

"You don't know what it means to me to hear Andy laugh, to see him so happy."

"Children are resilient. They can take a lot more than we give them credit for. Don't sell him short."

"I don't. It's just that he's not had a whole lot in his life so far to be happy about. But all that's changing now." She reached for his hand and brought it to her cheek. "You're part of it. A big part."

"You don't know anything about me," he said, uncomfortable with the tone of her voice, the warmth in her eyes.

"I know enough. I know you'd never lie to me."

He took her hand and turned it over to study it. "I might be an ax murderer, for all you know. Or an escaped prisoner. Anything."

A smile nipped at her lips. "I know you're a kind, gentle, decent man. A man who cares deeply. That's all I need to know."

Consumed with guilt, he didn't return the smile. He couldn't. The impossibility of his position multiplied with every day that passed.

Alone, in his rented room, he replayed every word between them. Relived every nuance of feeling. Brittany was making him feel things he hadn't known he was capable of feeling. Things like wanting a family. With Sherry, there'd been no talk of children. Her life revolved around her career as a designer and the trappings that went with it. He didn't feel he could ask her to give it up.

But things were different now. Because of Brittany.

"Don't you have to go to work today?" Clint asked, finding Brittany still grading papers at the kitchen table the following morning.

"One of my students is sick. I don't have another tutoring session until noon."

He poured two glasses of lemonade and handed one to her. "We need to talk."

She waited.

"I think you know how I feel. I want to be part of your life. And Andy's. I'm hoping you feel the same way?" He made a question of the last words.

She murmured an inarticulate sound.

"If I'm off track, let me know. But I need to hear it from you."

"You're not off track," she managed to say. "But I'm not ready—"

He stopped her. "I know that. I don't want to rush you. But I'm not a patient man. I need to know what you're feeling."

I love you. The words caught in her throat. She tried to say them but couldn't.

"I care about you. Very much. I wish I could make it more, but I can't." Her eyes begged him to understand.

He brushed the back of his hand against her cheek.

"That's enough. All I wanted was to know that I wasn't imagining what was happening between us."

"You weren't. But I'm afraid."

"Afraid of me?"

"No. Never. I'm afraid of commitment. Of getting hurt again."

"I would never hurt you. You or Andy. If you ever want me to go away, you'll have to tell me. Because nothing else could make me leave."

I don't want you to. She remained silent, wishing she had the courage to voice her thoughts aloud.

Warm hands cupped her face as he searched for an answer there.

She put a tentative hand to his cheek, touched by his declaration but still afraid to trust her own feelings. "Clint, you . . . me . . . how can you know for sure?"

"Because it's as much a part of me as breathing. *You're* a part of me."

"I don't want you to go." She at last found the strength to say the words.

"Brittany." Her name was a prayer, a plea, a promise.

"Clint, I need time," she said when he released her.

"I know. I didn't mean to rush you. It's been murder trying to keep my feelings to myself, and I had to hold you to make sure you were real. That what we feel for each other is real."

"It's real. More real than anything has ever been before."

"That's all I needed to know. We'll work everything else out. Together."

Clint's kiss feathered across her brow, a caress as gentle as a summer breeze. His lips traced the curve of her cheek, to pause at the lobe of her ear, and, finally, to rest upon her own.

Her mouth opened to receive his as a flower lifts its head to the sun, seeking its warmth. She marveled at her response to Clint's kisses.

When he eased away, Brittany drew a shaky breath. "I didn't know a kiss could be like this. Is it always like this for you?"

"Not always. Only when it's very, very special. Only with you."

"I didn't know," she said again.

"There's so much I want to share with you," he said softly, his lips nuzzling her hair. "But we won't rush it. We have all the time in the world." His words triggered the unwanted memory that he still faced his greatest hurdle: that of telling Brittany the truth.

"All the time in the world," she repeated, her eyes shining with the promise of tomorrow.

"Brittany," he said, forgetting for the moment that he'd promised her time. "Let me take care of you. You and Andy."

She pulled away regretfully. "I can't. Not yet."

"Why?"

"Until I know for sure what the future holds for Andy, I can't make promises. It would be unfair to ask you or any man to take on such problems."

"Do you think that'd make a difference to me?" he asked, stung by the implication. "I'm not like your ex-fiancé."

"I know you aren't. But I won't . . . I can't ask you. You've only seen Andy when he's feeling good. There were days, months even, when he couldn't move at all."

"But—"

She held up a hand as though to ward off further questions. "Please, Clint."

Frustration gnawed at his nerves as he acknowledged the promise he'd made. Uneasily, he remembered his deception. He couldn't press her for an answer until she knew the truth, and he was unwilling to take the chance of telling her until she trusted him further. A real catch-22 situation. But maybe he could help her another way.

"Isn't it about time you buried the past and forgave your parents?"

"It's not a matter of forgiving them," she said. "We see things differently. Too differently, I guess. I can't live with lies."

There it was again. Her obsession with the truth. "Don't deny yourself happiness because you're afraid someone will lie to you again."

"Who says I'm afraid?"

In answer, Clint took her hand in his, his fingers finding the erratic beat of her pulse. "That does."

"What makes you so smart?"

"I'm not. But occasionally I have flashes of perception.'' He slid her a teasing smile which she failed to return. He sobered quickly and said, ''I don't want to see you writing off a future for yourself. One that includes a husband and children. So far all I've heard is what you want for Andy. You haven't mentioned yourself once.''

''Is that so wrong?''

''It's wrong for you, and for Andy. What's going to happen when he grows up and leaves home? Are you sure you're not using him to avoid making a life for yourself?''

''Of course not,'' she flared.

''Don't get me wrong. I think you're doing a wonderful job with Andy. But it's time you started thinking of yourself too.''

Clint watched as her expressive face mirrored her thoughts. *Had he gone too far?*

He realized that by assuming guardianship of Andy, she'd taken on a huge responsibility, one most people would have avoided if they could. He didn't have the right to criticize her.

How she had managed to survive despite overwhelming problems filled him with a rush of admiration, and something more, for her. Some women would have been bitter at the cards life had dealt them, but not Brittany. She accepted each challenge with a calm he envied.

''You're saying I'm being selfish by concentrating on Andy?'' she asked.

''Not selfish. Just human. Andy's your sister's son;

he also has some problems. It's only natural that you'd make him the center of your life. I'm just asking you to let others in too. You're too loving, too giving to remain alone for the rest of your life."

"Maybe I don't want to marry. As for children, I have Andy. He's all I need." She crossed her arms in a defensive gesture.

He took her hands, bringing them to his lips where he gently nipped at her fingers. "Don't shut me out."

"I don't want to, but I'm so confused. I don't even know what I want sometimes."

"Join the rest of us then." *Funny.* He'd never thought of himself as confused before. He'd always known exactly what he wanted and gone after it. Until now. Until Brittany started making him want things like a home and family.

"You, too?"

"Me, too. Right now I may be the most mixed-up person I know. But maybe, just maybe, we can help each other, if you'll give us a chance."

She tried to look away, but he wouldn't let her. "I don't know."

"I want to help you, Brittany. If you'll trust me, we can reach for the rainbow. Together."

She fingered her pendant. "Rainbows don't last."

He felt her withdrawal and tried to ignore the rejection he felt at it. "They can. If we let them." He watched as confusion and doubt clouded her eyes. He ached to take away the fear that prevented her from accepting what he was offering.

"Clint . . ."

Her voice held a plea for time, understanding, and more. He heard it and respected it. For now.

oooChapter Six

"I wish you were my father."

Clint's head jerked up. The bent bicycle tire rim he held slipped from his hands and clattered to the ground.

Andy picked it up and handed it to him. "Can you fix it?"

The innocent question startled Clint almost as had the bombshell Andy had dropped only seconds earlier. He stalled, pretending to study the twisted metal. Andy had found a beat-up bicycle behind the barn. Though he couldn't ride it, he wanted a bike "like the other boys have."

"Huh? Oh, yeah. I think we can." Clint picked up a wrench at random and twisted it in his hands, stalling for time as he searched for an answer. "Andy."

The little boy looked up.

Clint chose his words carefully. "About what you said earlier. Nothing would make me happier than to be your father. If I were, I'd be so proud I'd bust. But sometimes we can't always have what we wish for." *That was the understatement of the year.*

"I know that." The matter-of-fact acceptance in the reed-thin voice tore at Clint as no amount of crying would have, and he wondered what kind of world they were living in for a child to sound so world-weary.

"I'm sure your dad loved you very much."

"Aunt Brittany says he did." Andy shook his head as he spoke. "I don't remember him real good."

Clint waited.

"He's in heaven now. At first, Grandma and Grandpa said he and Mom were on a trip. But then they told me Mom and Dad were dead. I think I knew before. But I didn't want to believe it. I cried when they told me. Does that make me a baby?"

Clint coughed to cover the thickness that lodged inside his throat. A soft hiss escaped his lips. Awkwardly, he drew Andy to him, wrapping his arms around him. The small body melted against his larger one. A muffled sob hung in the air as Andy burrowed further into Clint's arms.

"It's all right to cry," Clint said. "We all cry sometimes."

Andy swiped a small fist across his eyes before looking up at him. "Even you?"

Clint gave him a wry smile. "Even me." He handed Andy a handkerchief. "Blow."

After blowing his nose and sniffing loudly, Andy regarded Clint with skepticism. "You cry sometimes? Really?"

"Really. I bet you've heard crying is only for sissies. Crying only means you have feelings, that you care about others." How long it had been otherwise, he thought, acknowledging the barrenness of his own life up until now.

Until Brittany and Andy.

"I've never seen you cry," Andy said, his voice holding a question as well as a faint accusation.

"Can you keep a secret?" At the bobbing of the small towhead, Clint confided, "That's because I do it at night when no one else is around."

Andy's eyes grew wide. "Sometimes I cry then too. I don't want Aunt Brittany to see me. It makes her sad."

"Do you think she'd feel any better if she knew you were hurting and didn't tell her?"

"I s'pose not. Only . . . "

"Yeah, I know." Clint set Andy down, wiped the remaining tears from his cheeks, and gave him another quick hug. "Come on. You and I have a job to do."

Andy responded with a quick smile. "I like helping you."

"That's good. Because there's a lot of work around here to do. More than one *man* can do on his own. Another pair of hands is mighty welcome."

Andy's chest swelled with pride. "You can count

on me. Won't Aunt Brittany be surprised when she finds out that she's got two *men* to help out now?''

''Real surprised,'' Clint agreed, his grin slipping back into place.

''I'm glad you came here, Clint.''

The simplicity of the words touched him more than could anything more eloquent. ''I'm glad too.''

''I hope you can stay forever.''

''Forever is an awful long time. Maybe we ought to be happy with right now.''

Andy looked thoughtful. ''Okay.'' He bent his head to study his shoe lace. ''Clint, can right now sometimes last forever?''

Clint drew a deep breath. How had he gotten into a philosophical discussion with a six-year-old? ''Sometimes,'' he agreed cautiously.

''That's good. 'Cause that's what I think too.''

They spent the next half hour straightening the bent rim. If Clint dropped the pliers and confused the ratchet with the wrench, no one said anything.

''As good as new,'' he pronounced, giving the tire a final kick.

''Yeah. Just like new,'' Andy echoed. ''Only do you think we could . . . ''

''Could what?''

''Paint it blue.''

Clint looked at the canary-yellow paint job that the bike sported.

''Blue's a boy color,'' Andy explained. ''Yellow's a girl color.''

"You're right. If it's all right with your aunt, how about we go into town this afternoon and buy a can of spray paint?"

"Okay!"

Over lunch, he watched Andy, relieved to see that he was once more a little boy who was presently occupied with twirling his spaghetti around his fork. Gone was the pint-sized philosopher of an hour ago.

Unconsciously, he let out a sigh of relief, then looked about uneasily. Had Brittany noticed? His gaze met hers, held, then wavered.

She glanced significantly at Andy before bringing her gaze back to him. He read the question in her eyes.

I'll tell you later.

Brittany wondered what had caused Clint's preoccupation during lunch. Obviously it had something to do with Andy. Watching her nephew, who was currently trying to lick the last of the spaghetti sauce from his plate, she found it hard to believe that he could engender such distress.

"Aunt Brittany?"

Andy's voice claimed her attention.

"Clint says I'm a man now and can help him with the chores. Now you have two men around the house."

A suspicious wetness gathered in her eyes. She made a pretext of eating her spaghetti.

"Did you hear? I can help with the chores too. Clint said so."

"Great, Andy. Clint's right. I do have two men."

She bent to kiss his blond curls and straightened to find Clint's eyes on her.

Briskly she set about cleaning up. She commandeered the two ''men'' to help. Soon the three of them were splashing soap suds at each other. Not to be left out, Ralph cavorted through the kitchen, sliding on the slippery floor and adding to the general confusion.

Brittany swatted him gently with the broom, shooing him out of the house. He retreated to the porch after throwing her a reproachful look.

''Enough already,'' she cried as Clint snapped her with a wet towel in retaliation against her splashing him.

Glistening suds adorned his hair and clung to his eyelashes. *He's never looked more wonderful*, she decided. ''Had enough, huh?''

At that moment a cascade of water washed over him from behind. He whirled around to find Andy with a now-empty dishpan and a gleeful look.

She burst out laughing. ''I think you've been outclassed.''

''Outclassed nothing. I was hit from behind. A sneak attack.'' He grabbed Andy and swung him high above his head.

Andy's delighted squeals pierced the air. Brittany wiped the suds from her eyes and froze. The scene before her slowed to stills, each frame indelibly imprinted in her mind, as it unrolled before her.

Andy.

Clint.

The strong man swinging the small boy high, higher still in the air. She wanted to catch it, to save it, to store away for another day, a picture for the heart. A day when all she had was memories. The colors blurred through the veil of her tears. Through the bubble-dotted air she spotted a prism of color: a rainbow.

Again she wiped her eyes. This time, though, the wetness there tasted of salt.

The scene before her resumed its normal pace, and she shook herself out of her reverie, wondering if she'd just imagined it.

"Are you all right?" Clint asked.

"How can I be all right when you men have wrecked my kitchen?" She put her hands on her hips in pretended exasperation and glared at the two of them.

"We'll pitch in," he promised. "We'll have this place spic'n'span in no time."

"No time," Andy echoed.

Clint wielded a mop while Brittany tried to sop up as much water as she could with paper towels. Andy found a dry dish towel and started drying pots and pans.

"Can we go into town and buy paint?" Andy asked. When she didn't answer, he tugged on the pocket of her jeans. "Can we?"

"Can we what?"

He regarded her with ill-concealed impatience. "Go into town and buy paint for my bike?"

"Bike?" She felt Clint's gaze and caught herself in time before blurting out, "What bike?"

"Why not? As soon as we finish here—"

"It's just s'posed to be us guys," Andy said, clearly uncomfortable at having to point out that she wasn't invited.

"Oh. I see." For a moment, Brittany felt hurt. For the first time in two years Andy was excluding her. Then she laughed. "Of course it's just you guys. While you're doing that, I'll get caught up on some of my paper grading."

Andy caught her about her legs. "Thanks." Skinny arms tightened around her, threatening to topple her over.

Clint's arm steadied her as he whispered, "Sure it's all right?"

"I'm sure. What's this about a bike?"

"I'll tell you later." When she started to point out the obvious, he put a finger to her lips. She turned her attention to Andy and saw that his T-shirt was plastered to him. "Andy, maybe you'd better change your shirt before going into town."

"Gotcha." He gave her a wink before shuffling out of the room.

"Gotcha," she repeated and pulled a face. "Now, what's this about Andy having a bike?"

Quickly, Clint explained how they'd found an old bike behind the barn. "We got working on it and . . . " His expression beseeched her to understand.

"But—"

"But he can't ride it," he finished the thought for

her. "I know. What's more, he knows it. But it's important he have one. Like the other kids."

She nodded, grateful for his insight when her own had let her down. "Thanks. I didn't know."

He gently grazed her cheek with his knuckles. "Don't blame yourself. You're doing a great job with Andy."

"Thanks."

"What's wrong?"

"Nothing. Everything. Sometimes I'm scared of what's going to happen to him." There. She'd said it. She'd finally put into words the fear she'd lived with for so long.

Clint took her hands and covered them with his own. "You've got a right to be afraid."

"I'm sorry. I don't usually indulge in a pity party."

"Don't you think I know that?" He touched a finger to her lips, lifting the corners.

She managed a half-hearted smile and earned his approval.

"You'll be all right?"

"Sure. I'm tough, remember?" She flexed an imaginary muscle.

Clint laughed. "Remind me not to get into any fights with you. You'd slaughter me."

Their laughter broke the tension.

"I'm ready." Andy appeared in the hallway, halting anything Clint might have said.

"So you are," she agreed and resisted the urge to redo his efforts in dressing himself. With his shirt misbuttoned and shoes on the wrong feet, he made an endearing picture.

"Let's go, Clint," Andy said.

"Can you handle the rest of this by yourself?" Clint asked.

Brittany followed his gaze, taking in the still-damp floor, the sopping wet dish towels, the stack of pots and pans. "Without you two to help me, I'll be done in half the time," she said, only half joking.

Clint gave her a quick kiss. "We'll be back before you know it."

"That's what I'm afraid of." She snapped a towel at him, narrowly missing him.

"You'll pay for that later," he growled, the smile belying his fierce expression.

"C'mon, Clint." Andy tugged at his hand. "We need to go before the store closes."

"Sure thing, partner." They waved good-bye, and Brittany tried not to look as left out as she felt.

Alone, she gazed about, noting the puddles of water that had escaped the mop and the inexpertly washed pans that Andy had helped with. With a sigh, she began putting the place to rights. A faint whimpering from outside reminded her of Ralph.

She opened the front door. "Come on in, boy," she called. "Were you feeling left out too?" Absently, she scratched him behind the ears. He rolled over, clearly delighted with the unexpected attention.

Remembering Andy's plea that he and Clint go by themselves, she knew a certain urge to cry. Andy was growing up. And she had to learn to let go. Watching Clint with Andy this afternoon had made her acutely aware of how much he'd missed by not having a man in his life.

Two hours later, she threw down the magazine she'd been reading. After reading it for the fourth time, she acknowledged she had no more idea of what it said now than she had the first time.

"Where are they?" she wondered aloud. She'd long since finished grading the homework. Her imagination ran riot as dusk approached and there was still no sign of her "men" returning. Images of the Volkswagen laying in a gulch on its side with two lifeless bodies inside tormented her.

"Now, you're being silly," she told herself.

When she heard the unmistakable sputter of a creaky engine, she ran out to the porch.

Looking inordinately pleased with themselves, Clint and Andy climbed out of the car and walked toward the house.

Hands on her hips, she glared at them. "Where've you two been?"

"Uh-oh," Clint stage-whispered to Andy. "We're in for it now."

"Don't be mad. We've been shopping." Proudly, Andy held up a bag. "We got the paint plus some more stuff."

Brittany felt her anger melting under his excitement. "Come and tell me about it."

"Am I forgiven too?" Clint asked.

"I guess you are. Just tell me what took you so long. And how you both got so dirty," she added, noticing the Colorado-red clay that streaked their clothes.

"It's a long story. Why don't we start dinner while we talk?"

While Clint grilled hamburgers, Brittany tossed a salad.

"Well, are you going to tell me what you two were up to?" she asked when he didn't say anything.

"We bought the paint like we planned—"

"It was great. When we were at the store, some big kid started picking on Robbie Tolley. Clint told him to back off. That kid started swinging at Robbie, and Robbie ducked. Then Mr. Olson kicked us out of the store."

"It wasn't quite that bad," Clint said quickly. "By the time everybody was outside, we'd managed to break up the fight."

"Clint was awesome. He took us all over to the ball field and showed us the right way to fight."

Brittany looked from the excited boy to the sheepish man. "What?"

"I was teaching them to defend themselves," Clint said. He turned to Andy. "What did I tell you was the first thing you do if someone starts a fight?"

Andy frowned, clearly not liking this part of it. "First you try to work it out by com . . . com . . . "

"Compromising."

"That's right."

"I'm glad about that," Brittany said. "But what about teaching them how to fight?"

"How to defend themselves," Clint corrected. "Every kid needs to know how to do that."

"But—"

"Clint showed us how to duck, take a fall, all sorts of neat things."

"I still don't think—"

"You're not going to get all sissy, are you?" Andy asked.

At the crestfallen look on his face, she said, "Of course I'm not going to get sissy."

"Good. Let's eat. I'm starving."

"We're going to talk more about this later," she told him. "Go wash your hands and change your clothes."

"Do I have to?"

She swatted his bottom. "Yeah, you have to." She watched as he plodded off to his room. "I'm still not sure I like the idea of you teaching them that stuff," she said to Clint.

"Hey, you're not getting sissy on me, are you?"

"You men are all the same." She tried to sound severe but couldn't carry it off. A grin slid through her tightly pursed lips.

"That's better." Clint waited until Andy was out of earshot before explaining further. "I don't want you to get the wrong idea. A bigger kid was trying to pick a fight with Robbie. That didn't sit well with me, but I was *not* teaching the boys how to fight. I tried to give them some things to think about along with a lesson in self-defense. That's all.''

She laid a hand on his arm. "I know. I'm glad you were there to help Robbie. He's just now coming out of his shell. Something like that could set him back for months."

"He's a tough little guy. He'll do all right. I noticed he stuttered a bit."

"He has a learning disability which affects his ability to read and write. Somewhere along the way, he developed a stuttering problem too. Probably as a result of being teased by other kids."

"But you're helping him."

"I'm trying to. It's not easy when he's been conditioned to think of himself as dumb."

"If anyone can do it, you can."

Brittany felt her face heat under his praise. Another thought chased the pleasure away and caused a frown to appear. "What about Andy? All he can think about now is fighting."

"He's a little boy. Give him time. And don't sell him short. He was impressed with a couple of showy moves. Nothing more."

"I don't want him thinking that fighting is the way to solve problems."

"Neither do I. That's what I was trying to show him and the others—that fighting is not a solution to anything." Clint cupped her face between her hands. "Sometimes there are fights you can't walk away from.

When that time comes, I want my . . . Andy to be prepared.''

What had he been about to say? she wondered. My son?

"How do you know so much?" she asked, refusing to ask the question that hovered in the air. "I feel like I'm walking a tightrope with Andy. I don't want to be over-protective, but—"

He slid an arm around her waist. "But you worry anyway."

Warmth trickled through her at his nearness, nearly robbing her of the ability to think. "Yeah. I do. That's what mothers . . . and aunts . . . do best. At least this one."

He lowered his head to cover her lips with his own. "And this is what I do best."

Her lips parted to receive the sweetest kiss she'd ever known.

She'd known it was coming. She welcomed it.

When he released her, she looked up at him to surprise a look of infinite tenderness in his eyes. *Was there sadness also*? She wanted to ask what had caused it, but she was afraid. A chill scampered down her spine, and she shivered.

"Cold?" Clint drew her closer.

"No. Yes. I mean—"

The scraping of Andy's shoes on the floor alerted her that they were no longer alone. She started to pull away from Clint's arms, but he held her secure. "It won't hurt for him to see us together."

Brittany felt her face heat with color as Andy gave them a curious glance before asking, "Can we make some ice cream tonight?"

"Ice cream?" She laughed, marveling at the workings of the mind of a six-year-old. "It's pretty late. It takes a long time to make ice cream." She looked at Clint, caught his chuckle, and gave in. "Well, I guess if we got started right now—"

"Yippee!"

"Dinner first."

"Could we have ice cream for dinner?"

"Absolutely not." Seeing his disappointment, she added, "It's hamburgers."

In record time, Andy polished off two burgers and, under protest, a bite of salad. Brittany had barely finished her first hamburger before he shouted, "It's ice cream time!"

Andy's war cry galvanized her into action, and she pulled the ice cream maker from the cupboard. Rummaging through the refrigerator, she found cream and eggs. "It'll have to be vanilla."

"Next to chocolate, that's my favorite."

"Mine, too," Clint seconded.

After the ingredients were poured into the stainless steel tub surrounded by ice, he began cranking.

Under his steady rhythm, the mixture began to thicken. "Hope my arm holds out." He flexed his shoulders and gave a convincing imitation of someone in great pain.

Brittany insisted they share the cranking and gamely

took her turn at it. She grimaced when the handle creaked and groaned under her efforts.

Clint watched for a moment before gently setting her aside. "Once it reaches this stage, it gets harder to crank. How about you and Andy get me some more ice?" The cranking once again resumed its smooth rhythm under his slow but steady pace.

An hour later, they tasted the homemade treat.

Finishing his bowl immediately, Andy smacked his lips and demanded seconds.

"One scoop," she said, smiling as she dipped a large spoonful into his bowl. She turned to Clint. "Has your arm recovered?"

He grinned. "I think I'll survive." He scraped the bottom of the bowl. "Makes the store-bought stuff taste like cotton, doesn't it?" He held out his bowl for more.

Smiling, Brittany refilled it. "Nothing like it. I could eat this all day." She brought her spoon to her lips and slurped it appreciatively. "It's a good thing we don't make it too often. I'd be a butterball in no time flat."

"Somehow I don't think you have to worry about that."

She flushed. "I wasn't fishing for compliments."

He covered her hand with his own. "I know that."

"Can I have one more scoop?" Andy asked.

She started to answer when Clint intervened. "Too much and you'll likely have nightmares. How 'bout we put the rest in the freezer and you can have some for dinner tomorrow?'' He looked at Brittany, who nodded.

Andy sneaked a look at the clock. ''Would you read me a story, Clint?''

Brittany recognized the ploy for what it was. ''Bedtime for you. It's already an hour after your bedtime.''

''But—''

''No buts.''

''Come on, slugger,'' Clint said. He scooped Andy up and swung him under his arm. ''All right if I do the honors tonight?''

''Sure,'' she said, and blinked to keep back the tears. She put a hand to her cheek and felt the wetness there. Andy had never been happier. *Neither have I*, she acknowledged, as she began clearing the table.

A ripple of laughter erupted from the bedroom, and she smiled to herself as she imagined the horseplay that her ''two men'' were engaging in.

''He's a great kid,'' Clint said after he returned a few minutes later. ''One any man would be proud of.''

''You'd think so, wouldn't you?'' A sad smile played at her lips. ''My fiancé didn't think so. His exact words were that he didn't want to be stuck with someone else's brat.''

''He was a jerk.''

''Yeah,'' she said. ''He was.''

Clint came to stand behind her. ''Let's sit down,'' he said, leading her to the sofa. ''We need to talk.''

A little apprehensive at the tone of his voice, she

nodded. When they were settled on the sofa, she looked at him expectantly.

"Andy and I had quite a conversation today," he began. Quietly, he repeated what Andy had told him.

She couldn't help it. Tears pooled in her eyes for the second time in as many minutes. She scrubbed at them with the back of her hand.

"Don't cry, honey." Clint gathered her into his arms, rocking her back and forth as he would a small child, all the while murmuring soothing words.

She let herself soak up the comfort he was offering, the strength that was so much a part of him. With an effort, she pulled away.

Clint must have sensed the conflict warring within her, for he released her rather than urging her to stay in his arms.

She looked at his face and knew she'd hurt him.

"I knew there was something," she said when the tears had stopped. "I just didn't expect this."

"It's only natural." At her uncomprehending look, he explained, "That he'd respond to the first man he's had a chance to get close to."

"Oh." She'd hoped he meant something else. Something more.

He groaned. "I'd give my right arm if Andy were mine. If you were mine."

They were bordering on dangerous territory. Right now, her concern had to be for Andy. She focused on that. It was safer. "What do you suggest we do?"

"I tried to tell Andy that sometimes what we want doesn't always come true. I think he understood."

"If he's started thinking about a father, I'm glad it was you." Brittany spoke impulsively. Immediately, she flushed. "I mean—"

"I know what you meant. For the record, I'm glad it was me too."

"Sometimes I don't feel any older than Andy. I wish for things that can't come true."

"Maybe, just maybe, some things can," he whispered and kissed her.

His kiss deepened, stealing her breath, and she gasped for air when he lifted his head. It was only then that the impact of his words sank in.

"Clint?" She raised questioning eyes to his.

An unfathomable expression settled over his face, making her disinclined to question him further.

"Goodnight, my love." He brushed his lips across her forehead. "We'll figure this out. Together."

She watched as he let himself out, closing the door behind him.

"My love," he'd said. Was she really?

A sense of being cherished stayed with her long after he'd gone to bed. It wrapped around her like a warm blanket. There was no reason to feel this way, she told herself. She didn't *need* a man in her life. She'd been without one for too long, taking care of herself and Andy long before Clint had appeared.

Still, she hugged his words to her. *Together.* Dare she reach out to grab the happiness he offered? She imagined she could see the colors of the rainbow, bold and bright, beckoning to her over the horizon.

But a cloud loomed larger, gray and threatening, as the past came back to haunt her. Memories, still painful and raw, did not vanish so easily. She wiped her hands across her eyes, hoping that by the simple action she could erase them once and for all.

She couldn't deny the intense sweetness that filled her whenever she thought of Clint. It colored her thoughts and her dreams with a quiet happiness she hadn't known was possible.

A sense of foreboding tinged her happiness, though, as she thought of the future. A future without Clint. It loomed lonely and dark. Bleakly, she wondered if she would ever be the same once he had left.

Somehow she doubted it. She doubted it very much.

Chapter Seven

M_{r.} Tolley paced across the porch, shuffling his hat back and forth in his hands.

Brittany saw him and suppressed a groan. She was hot and tired after having to walk the last mile home when her car stalled. The hour tutoring session with a homebound student had stretched into two, and all she wanted to do was soak in a tub of hot water. Still, she schooled her lips into a smile.

"Did you want to see me, Mr. Tolley?" she asked as she climbed the porch steps.

"Yes, ma'am, I did."

"Would you like to sit down?" She indicated the old-fashioned swing.

He shook his head. "I'd rather stand, ma'am, if it's all the same with you."

"Of course. Would you mind if I sit?" She sank wearily onto the swing and pushed her hair off her forehead.

"No, ma'am." He cleared his throat, clearly uncomfortable. "Miz Howard, you heard what happened in town yesterday?"

"Yes, I did." She waited.

"It's just like I said it would be. Kids picking on my Robbie. Because he's different. It ain't no different than the barnyard. The hens know when one of them is smaller, weaker, than the rest. Then they start to peck at it and don't stop until they've pecked it to death."

Brittany heard the anguish in his voice, the despair he did not try to hide. "I'm more sorry than I can say that it happened, Mr. Tolley. But didn't Robbie tell you what happened after that?"

He looked uncomfortable. "Yeah. He said something about your handyman stepping in and then showing the boys the right way to fight."

"It wasn't like that," Brittany said quietly. "Clint— Mr. Bradley—showed the boys how to defend themselves, not how to fight. There's a big difference."

"Yeah, well, that's as may be. But it don't change nothing. That kid was picking on my Robbie, all because he started at that school you're so dad-blamed proud of. You told me it would be different. Well, it ain't. It ain't no different than any of the others." He wiped a beefy hand across his eyes before digging into his pocket for a handkerchief.

"Mr. Tolley, I wish I could tell you that people will automatically change, but they won't. Kids like the one who was picking on Robbie are always going to be around. At least, they will until someone teaches them differently. That's what we're trying to do at Stansberry. But we can't do it if parents withdraw their children from school without giving it, or the school, a chance." Brittany took a deep breath. "We need parents like you. And kids like Robbie. Have you asked him how he feels about it?"

Mr. Tolley shifted his gaze from her. "Yeah. I asked."

"And?"

"He wants to keep going to school," he admitted.

"What do you want, Mr. Tolley?"

"I want my boy to be happy. Ain't nothing I wouldn't do for him. It ain't been easy since his mother ran out on us. But I've done the best I could. You gotta believe that."

"I do," she said softly. "I also believe in Robbie."

Mr. Tolley rubbed his jaw. "Robbie likes you."

"I like him too," she said softly.

"We'll give it another try," he said at last. "I appreciate your handyman stepping in, like he did. But I don't hold with teaching kids how to fight. I don't have much schooling, but I know fighting won't solve nothing. I've been in enough of them to know better."

"I agree, Mr. Tolley," a voice from behind Brittany said. "Fighting won't solve anything." Clint stepped farther into the room and came to stand beside Brittany, placing a hand on her shoulder.

Mr. Tolley stood. "Guess you'd be Bradley."

Clint held out his hand. "That's right."

After a moment's hesitation, the other man took it and shook it, pressing it hard. "Thanks for sticking up for Robbie the way you did. I'm glad you was there."

"So am I. He's a good boy."

"That he is." He gave Clint a measuring glance. "If there's anything I can ever do for you, you let me know, and it'll be done." He shifted his attention back to Brittany. "Miz Howard, you're a good teacher. I've got no quarrel with you. I just wanted you to know how I feel."

Brittany held out her hand. "Thanks for coming by, Mr. Tolley. We're going to help Robbie. Together. I promise."

He jammed his hat on his head. "Thank you for your time, ma'am."

Clint slipped an arm around Brittany's waist as they watched Mr. Tolley drive away in a battered pickup. "He really cares about his son, doesn't he?"

She nodded. "He's like any parent. He can't bear to see his child hurting."

"I hope he realizes how lucky he is that Robbie has you for a teacher."

"I'm the lucky one. I get to work with kids like Robbie. I won't pretend that it's easy, because it's not. But when I see a child who's never read before start reading or Robbie talk without stuttering, I know it's all worthwhile.''

A shadow crossed her face as she thought of all the children who needed help.

"Robbie's one of the lucky ones. He was diagnosed early enough to get help when it can make a difference. More importantly, he has a father who genuinely cares. But there are so many more children who need the extra time, the extra bit of love that their parents can't give to them because they're so caught up in just trying to survive.

"I wish there were some kind of support group in this area for families with children with special needs. If just one parent could hear that other families are going through some of the same problems, maybe it would encourage him to keep trying.''

She hesitated, wondering if she should share her dream with him of building a center where parents and families could come for counseling. So far that's all it was—a dream.

"What is it?" Clint asked when she paused.

"Just an idea I've had for a long time that nothing will ever come of.''

"Hey, that doesn't sound like the Brittany I know. She wouldn't let anything stop her if she really believed in something." He grinned. "Give.''

"So many families with special-needs children need counseling. But a lot of them can't afford it. Not on a long-term basis, anyway. I'd also like to start a therapy group for parents, a place where they can share their frustrations and their tears. Even the small things, like having a child be rejected for a school soccer team because he can't tell his right from his left, can seem overwhelming when you're all alone.''

"Sounds like a great idea."

"Like most good ideas, it'll probably never get off the ground for want of money." She tried to smile but failed. "I've babbled on for too long. You must be bored stiff."

"Never. I'd like to hear more."

"Really?"

"Really."

Warming to her subject, she said, "I've seen the discouragement that comes when a mother finally admits to herself that her child is never going to be able to do all the things she dreamed of. And what can happen when she learns there are others out there with the same feelings, the same problems, who have coped and raised happy children in spite of everything. It can make all the difference."

Clint kissed her lightly. "You're something else, you know that?"

She threw off her introspective mood and smiled at him. "What I know is that I'm hot, tired, and hungry."

He chuckled. "I see where Andy gets his appetite from."

"Hey, I just walked two miles. I've got a right to be hungry. Give me five minutes to shower, and I'll start dinner."

Andy wandered onto the porch. "Did I hear something about dinner?"

Clint and Brittany burst out laughing.

The rest of the evening was spent playing Chutes and Ladders, with Andy the clear winner.

"No fair," Clint said when Andy won his third game. "I never even passed the first ladder."

"Too bad," Brittany said. "Pay up. We all agreed. Loser has to give Ralph a bath."

"Okay," he said, "but can we make it tomorrow? It's Saturday. Giving Ralph a bath will take the whole day."

"I've heard of sermons that were drier than dust, but . . ." Clint gestured expressively.

Brittany tried not to smile but it slipped through anyway. "Reverend Crews does tend to go on, doesn't he?"

"Just a bit."

They'd just come home from church. Andy had disappeared into his room to play, leaving Brittany and Clint alone. She kicked off her shoes and sank onto the couch. Her poppy-red sundress billowed out around her.

Clint settled beside her. "Feet hurt?"

She nodded, grimacing toward the high-heels. "The price we pay for vanity."

The little-boy grin that appeared only rarely skidded across Clint's lips. "Let me." He took her feet in his lap and gently began to massage them.

She sighed her pleasure. "You could go into the massage business if you decide to give up carpentry."

Clint didn't smile as she'd expected; instead, a shadow crossed his face.

"Hey, I was only joking."

"I know." He continued kneading the soles of her feet. "I have to go to Denver."

"When?"

"Today. I've put it off too long as it is."

What was it? she wanted to ask. "For how long?"

"I'm not sure. Not more than a couple of days at the most."

She tried not to let her disappointment show. "Business?" she asked casually.

"I need to check on some things."

The fact that he hadn't given a direct answer didn't escape her notice, but she didn't question him. She didn't have the right. "I'll miss you."

"I hope so."

"Do you want me to pack you a lunch?"

"If it's not too much trouble."

She slathered slices of bread with mustard and added sliced roast beef, topping it off with shredded lettuce, all the while trying to ignore the fact that they sounded like strangers.

"Thanks." He took the sack and kissed her good-bye. "Hey, I won't be gone that long."

She summoned a smile. "I know."

The rest of the day dragged, with each hour seeming longer than the last. Brittany cleaned cabinets, polished furniture, and even dusted under the beds. But nothing erased the loneliness. *Is this how it's going to be when he's gone for good?* she wondered.

She'd avoided making a commitment, using the excuse that she didn't want to burden Clint with a ready-made family, especially one with their special problems. Now she knew she'd been lying to herself: It hadn't been out of concern for Clint, but plain, old-fashioned fear. Well, she wasn't afraid anymore.

When Clint returned, she was going to tell him how she felt. If he still wanted her and Andy, then . . . She didn't let herself think beyond that.

Denver hadn't changed. Its famous brown cloud blanketed the city. A cacophony of noise assaulted his eardrums wherever he went. But he could live with those. What he couldn't live without was Brittany. If he'd thought he could, a half day away convinced him he'd been wrong.

He spent four hours at the office, catching up on the never-ending paperwork before driving to the site of the new hospital. Bradley Construction had won the bid on the hospital. Today was the ground-breaking ceremony.

For the first time in weeks, he was wearing a suit and tie. He tugged at the unaccustomed tightness around his neck. If Brittany could see him now—

"Brittany," he whispered, wishing he was with her right now, "I love you. Please try to understand."

The hushed prayer fell unanswered. An inner cold

cut through to the very bone, contrasting with the lingering heat of the day. Fear skittered along his backbone when he contemplated what he had to do.

Stop it, he ordered himself. He'd make her see that his job was just that—a job. Whether he was a handyman or president of a multimillion-dollar firm, it made no difference in how he felt about her. That was all that mattered. He'd tell Brittany everything.

She'd be angry, all right. He didn't doubt that, but they'd work through it. He'd convince her that they belonged together. Then he'd ask her to marry him. The decision made, he felt as though a great weight had been lifted from his chest.

Two hundred miles away, Brittany felt a faint chill, a cold hand tracing a path down her spine. She wrapped her arms around herself, trying to ward off the uneasy sensation that something was wrong. She looked at the letter bearing the return address of Denver Children's Hospital once more. She wished Clint was here. Perhaps he could help her make the toughest decision a parent could face.

The old saying, "Someone's walking over my grave," came to mind, and she shivered again.

Her thoughts strayed to Clint. *Was he all right? Where was he? Would he be back?*

"Clint," she murmured. "I need you. Please, hurry back."

*   *   *

Clint drove quickly, anxious to put as many miles between himself and Denver as possible. He arrived after 11 P.M. He knocked lightly, not wanting to wake her if she was already in bed. A compelling need to see her kept him at the porch even when no light appeared.

Just when he would have turned away, a light switched on in the kitchen.

"Clint?"

"Yes."

The door opened immediately. Brittany stood there, silhouetted by the moonlight. "I was hoping you'd make it back tonight."

Clint grinned as he slipped his arm around her. He closed the door behind him. "Miss me?"

"Do you need me to tell you?"

"No. But I like to hear you say it."

"I missed you," she said softly, and wound her arms around his neck. "Too much."

"I feel like I've been away forever."

"It seems like you have." She sighed at the butterfly kisses which skipped along her neck.

"What's that?" he asked.

"Lavender."

"It smells good. Like something my grandmother used to wear."

"I'm glad you like it."

"I like it all right. I like everything about you, Brittany. You make me believe in things like happily-ever-afters. I can't imagine a life without you in it." He flushed. It was a long speech for a man who usually shunned pretty words.

A profound contentment pervaded him. He felt he could stay this way forever, with Brittany locked in his arms. Finally, he loosened his hold, turning her so that their eyes met.

Tell her now, a voice whispered. *Tell her. She'll understand, and then nothing will stand between you.*

"Brittany, I have—"

"What's going on?" Andy shuffled out of the bedroom, rubbing sleepily at his eyes. He saw Clint and let out a yelp. "Clint's home. Why didn't you tell me?" He turned reproachful eyes upon her.

"I'm sorry, honey." Blushing, she extricated herself from Clint's arms and went to Andy. "Clint just got in. It was so late, we didn't want to wake you."

"That's okay. I'm glad you're home, Clint."

"Me too, Andy." He knew a frustration that they'd been interrupted, but also relief. *Admit it, you're glad to put it off a while longer.* Clint joined Brittany and stage-whispered, "All right for a piggyback ride back to bed?"

She smiled in answer.

Careful of the braces, Clint hoisted the small boy up on his back. Thin arms wrapped themselves around his neck as Andy clung to his neck.

In a few minutes, Clint returned. "He wrangled a promise out of me for a picnic tomorrow. Think we can manage it?"

"I have a million things to do around here. There's

the laundry, the new slipcovers I was going to make for the couch, and a week's worth of papers to grade. You know what? I don't want to do a single one of them.''

''That's what Saturdays are for—to play hooky.'' He used the same wheedling tone Andy had just a few minutes earlier.

She tried to give him a reproving look and failed. ''You're as bad as Andy is.''

''I'll take that as a compliment. Now, how about it? Are we going to have that picnic or not?''

''You twisted my arm.''

He held her gently, savoring the feel of her, the scent of her hair, the essence that was Brittany. He led her to the sofa and pulled her down beside him.

''I love you,'' he said. ''More than I thought possible.''

''I love you too,'' she said, the little hitch in her voice doing funny things to his heart.

''I'm not leaving, Brittany,'' he promised. ''Not unless you ask me to.''

''I know you can't stay here forever.''

He read the question in her eyes. ''I'm making some changes in my life. That's why I had to go away. I may have to leave again. But I'll be back. I'll always be back.''

''As long as we love each other, we'll work everything else out.''

''No one can promise the future. But I can promise

to love you as much as it's humanly possible to love someone." He turned her to face him. "Trust me?"

She nodded. "Always."

He curved her to him and marveled at how well they fit each other. Her head, tucked inside the arch of his neck, rested under his chin. He inhaled deeply, delighting in the sweet scent of her hair and skin, a soap-and-water freshness that was hers alone.

We'll work everything else out. He prayed he could make her words come true.

Chapter Eight

They spent the day fishing in the creek that separated Brittany's property from the neighboring one, a lazy day with the heat shimmering off the water and the chirping of the birds a natural symphony.

"Aunt Brittany, Clint, I got one." Andy held his line high, a speckled fish dangling from it.

"Good going," Clint called back. He left his own line propped on a rock and went to help Andy detach the rainbow trout. "Looks like he's a couple of pounds at least. We can fry him for tonight's dinner if it's all right with your aunt."

They turned expectantly toward Brittany. She laughed. "As long as I don't have to clean him."

"Girls don't like to do that stuff," Andy confided to Clint in a low tone.

"You're right," Clint agreed solemnly. "But they do other things we like, don't they?"

"Yeah, I guess you're right." Andy frowned, considering. "Aunt Brittany's all right for a girl."

Clint smothered a laugh. "I think so too."

Brittany tried hard to look indignant, but ended up laughing. "I'm glad I have my uses."

"Oh, you do," Clint assured her. "You definitely do." He gave her an unmistakable leer and twisted an imaginary mustache.

"Hey, Clint, you're not fishing," Andy accused. "You can talk to Aunt Brittany anytime."

Clint slanted her a rueful look. "Looks like I have my orders." Obediently, he trotted back to his spot and picked up his pole, casting the line into the stream. He leaned lazily against the trunk of a tree, impossibly handsome in faded jeans and a soft flannel shirt.

The dappled sunlight, peeking through the branches, warmed her face as Brittany studied him. In his relaxed state, the hard lines which furrowed his forehead and framed his mouth all but disappeared. A shank of light gilded his nut-brown hair with gold. His rolled-up sleeves bared his arms, now bronzed by working under the Colorado sun. Fine hairs matted his forearms, disappearing under his shirt sleeves.

A smile teased her lips as a gentle breeze lulled her into a light sleep.

Clint watched as Brittany relaxed under the tree, letting her line go limp. Quietly, he removed the pole from her hand. A few curls had escaped the rubber band holding back her hair, and he brushed them away from her face. He grazed his lips across hers, then leaned back to study her.

The worry he'd seen in her eyes had lessened, and the strain around her mouth had eased. He wished she'd tell him what was bothering her. He'd seen it appear this morning as she read a letter when she thought he wasn't looking.

With a lingering look at her slightly parted lips, he returned to the rock where Andy waited impatiently. Clint cast his line into the water with practiced ease.

"Wow, could you teach me how to do that?" Andy asked. Since his first cast, he'd had trouble keeping his line untangled.

"Sure thing." Clint reeled his line in and showed Andy how to flex his wrist while casting. "Keep it smooth," he said. "Let it glide out."

On his first try, Andy fumbled, twisting his line.

"It's all right," Clint told him. "Everybody has a hard time at first."

A frown puckered Andy's face as he concentrated on his task. After several more attempts, he asked Clint to show him again. This time, he succeeded in casting as Clint had demonstrated. Companionably, they fished there before moving to another place. Every once in a while, Clint glanced over at Brittany.

She looked more rested than he'd ever seen her. Frowning, he remembered she'd had little reason lately to relax. Right now, she looked like a young girl, her face innocent of makeup and freckle-kissed by the sun.

He drew his gaze away from her when Andy shouted his name. A jerk on his line alerted him to the fish pulling on it.

"Get the net," he called to Andy.

Andy grabbed the net and started to enter the stream, then looked down at his braces. His shoulders drooped and, wordlessly, he handed the net to Clint.

"Here." Clint handed the pole to Andy. He splashed into the stream and scooped up the speckled rainbow trout dangling from the line.

"Good job reeling him in," Clint called.

"I didn't do anything," Andy said dully.

"I couldn't have done it without you." Clint looked at the fish. "He's pretty big, but not as big as yours."

Methodically, he removed the fish from the hook, pretending not to notice Andy's dejection.

"I wanted to catch him in the net," Andy said.

"I know. But you did your part. You reeled him in. Without you, I'd have lost him."

"But—"

"But nothing." Clint touched the metal braces that supported Andy's legs. "I won't say I know how you feel because I don't. Someday you may not need your braces. But right now you do."

"I know. It's just sometimes I forget and then something happens and I remember . . . "

"Hey, sometimes I forget too. Know what that means?"

Andy shook his head.

"It means you take care of yourself so well that most

people won't give your braces a second thought. Unless you do."

"You think so?"

"I *know* so. How 'bout we get back to work?"

"Okay."

Together, they caught five more fish, though none measured as big as the first catch of the day.

Brittany was dreaming. An annoying insect buzzed around her head, interrupting the fantasy. Her lips pouted at the intrusion, and she twisted around, searching for a more comfortable position. She swiped at the insistent fly hovering above her face, and settled back to enjoy the dream. She and Clint . . . There it was again, and she absently swatted at it.

"Wake up, sleepyhead." Clint tickled her with the feather.

He caught the hand she raised and brought it to his lips. She awoke with a start at the kiss he pressed on her palm.

"What!" she sputtered and glared at him.

"Must have been some dream you were having." Clint slid down next to her, casually draping an arm around her shoulders.

Was the man a mind reader? "How did you know I was dreaming?"

"Lucky guess."

The warmth in his gaze caused her to flush. She pulled herself up and wrapped her arms around her knees. "We . . . uh . . . probably ought to do something with those fish," she said, and immediately felt foolish.

He sat beside her. "You're right." He shaded his eyes against the sun as he scanned the bank for Andy. "Hey, Andy. What do you say we pack up? Your aunt's anxious to fry us up a mess of fish for dinner."

She poked his arm. "That wasn't what I meant."

He grinned. "I know."

Grumbling good-naturedly, she helped him pack up the fishing gear.

"Do we have to go?" Andy asked for the sixth time.

" 'Fraid so, sport," Clint said. "We've been here for three hours already. I'm afraid Brittany's getting sunburned."

She felt her face, surprised at the warmth of her cheeks. "How long did I sleep?"

"Just a couple of hours."

"Why didn't you wake me?"

Clint grinned. "You looked so cute sleeping, I couldn't bear to wake you up."

"I guess I was a little tired."

"Is something bothering you?"

Brittany resisted the temptation to unburden herself to him. She still had to sort it out in her own mind first. Perhaps then she could share the problem she'd been wrestling with ever since she'd opened the letter from Children's Hospital yesterday.

She looked up, aware he was still waiting for an answer. "I—"

"Hey, I thought we were going to cook my fish," Andy broke in.

"Sorry, Sport," Clint said. "We're coming." He turned back to Brittany. "You were about to say?"

"Nothing," she answered too brightly. "Andy's right. We'd better eat before I starve to death." As though on cue, her stomach growled, confirming her words.

Clint gave her a searching look. She thought she read disappointment in his eyes. The moment passed, and when she looked again, she saw only a teasing light as he tousled Andy's hair.

"If I'd known I was taking two such hungry people fishing, I'd have suggested we make a campfire and cook our fish over it."

"Can we?" Andy asked at once.

Brittany threw Clint a doubtful look. Her camping skills were next to nil. "I don't know—"

"Please, Clint," Andy begged.

"What do you say?" Clint asked, turning to Brittany. "I used to be a Boy Scout. I think I can still get a fire going."

She looked at Andy's sunburned nose and skinned knees and knew he'd never been happier. "I'll start gathering firewood."

Andy threw his arms around her neck. "This is the bestest day in my life. And you're the bestest aunt in the world." He scuffled off to find kindling.

"Andy's right."

"Right about what?"

"You're the bestest aunt in the world." Surprised at the sudden tears that gathered in her eyes, he drew her close to him. "Hey, what's this? That's supposed to be a compliment."

"I know," she said, using the balls of her hands to wipe away the tears. "Sometimes I don't feel like the bestest. I feel scared and wonder if I'm doing the right thing."

Clint gently pushed her back down on the rock and then dried her tears with his handkerchief. "Okay. What's this all about?"

"Are you bucking to be the world's oldest Boy Scout?"

"No. Just a friend. Now, give."

Haltingly, she told him about the letter. "Dr. Jeffers thinks there's a chance Andy may be able to walk. *If* he has this operation. If he doesn't, his legs will deteriorate until he won't be able to walk at all, even with crutches." She shook her head. "I don't know what to do."

"There's more, isn't there? Besides the risks, I mean."

She nodded. "I don't know if I can put Andy through another six weeks in the hospital. Last time, he begged me not to make him go there again." Tears trickled down her cheeks as she remembered.

"I wish you'd told me about this sooner."

"I wanted to. It's just I'm not used to having . . ."

"Having what?"

"Someone who cares what happens to me—to us." The admission cost her dearly.

Now it was Clint who turned away. He shifted so

he was no longer looking at her, staring instead at the river. She followed his gaze. The water mirrored the sky, now gray and cloudy, a reflection of her own turbulent feelings.

Brittany touched his arm. "Clint?"

"Sorry," he muttered. "I was . . . thinking."

"I'm sorry. I shouldn't have laid all this on you. I didn't have any right to expect you—"

"You had every right," he cut in, surprising her with his intensity.

"I don't understand."

"It's me. I care about what happens to you. You and Andy. You have to believe me."

Brittany couldn't doubt his sincerity. Then why had he turned away from her? Could it be he was as afraid of commitment as she was?

"What will you do—about the operation?" he asked after long seconds had passed.

"I don't know," she said, pressing her fingers against her temples in an effort to relieve the pressure mounting there. "I have a while before I have to decide. The doctor warned me most parents go back and forth a number of times before trying to make a decision like this."

"I wish I knew what to tell you. If I could help . . . "

"You already have. More than you'll ever know. Just by listening. It's been a long time since I've been able to share things with anyone. It helps having someone who will listen while I try to make sense of all this."

He wanted to do so much more. His deceit washed over him, and inwardly, he cursed the role in which he'd cast himself.

"Hey, Brittany, Clint," Andy called as he picked his way over the riverbank, using his crutches carefully to test for soft spots. "What's taking you so long? I thought we were going to eat."

Brittany looked up with a guilty start. She put a hand to her cheeks, hoping her tears had dried and that Andy wouldn't notice the redness around her eyes.

She darted a glance at Clint. "We're coming. You know us old folk. It takes us a little longer," she joked feebly.

"You're not old," Andy said loyally. "Not real old, anyway."

"Gee, thanks." She shared a rueful look with Clint.

"Come on, Grandma," he teased, offering her a hand up.

She let him pull her to her feet and felt as though she'd come home when he drew her against his chest. She rested there, savoring the warmth of his arms as they wrapped around her, wishing she could stay there forever.

Later that night, Brittany replayed their conversation. A sweet warmth enveloped her as she remembered his concern for her and Andy. She loved Clint. Loved him more than she thought possible.

The following morning, she emerged from her room, her hair neatly plaited into a braid, her face scrubbed.

She found Andy happily slurping down a bowl of cereal and watching TV.

He looked up briefly from the screen, where robotic cops chased their counterparts. "Hi." Before she could answer, he'd returned to his show.

"Hi, yourself," she said, smiling at the milk mustache that lined his upper lip. "How long have you been up?"

"Just a little while. Clint and me made pancakes." Proudly, he pointed to the stack of hotcakes on his plate swimming in a pool of buttery syrup.

Clint took a carton of eggs from the refrigerator. "I was just getting ready to cook some eggs. How would you like yours? Scrambled, scrambled, or scrambled?"

"Scrambled would be great."

"Good choice. Want some cheese with them?"

"Fine," she replied absently, intent on watching Andy. He hobbled to the TV to turn the channel. *His braces hardly slow him down at all. Maybe he doesn't really need the operation.* There were so many things that could go wrong. Did she have the right to take that risk with his life?

Later, when Andy had taken Ralph outside, she picked up a dish towel, twisting it in her hands.

Clint whistled while scrubbing the mountain of pots and pans he and Andy had managed to use.

"About last night," she began, and then stopped. "Thank you for being there."

"I always want to be there for you," he said quietly.

"I want the same thing," she said. "I love you."

He turned to stare at her, a frown wedged between his brows. "You don't have to say that."

"I want to. I love you. I have for a long time." She felt like a tremendous weight had been lifted from her chest.

He covered the short distance between them and closed his arms around her. "You don't know how long I've waited to hear you say that."

"I'm glad you waited." She drew a shaky breath. "I feel . . . I don't know what I feel."

"Brittany, there's something I want to tell you."

She put a finger to his lips. "Can it wait? I feel like doing something wild and wonderful." She spread her arms.

A smiled nudged his lips upward.

Andy looked from Brittany to Clint, then back to Brittany. "Did something happen?" he asked, shuffling toward them.

She smiled. "Why do you ask?"

"You look different." He touched her face. "All shiny."

"Is that good?" she asked. "I hope so because I *feel* different. A good kind of different."

"I'll never understand how I got so lucky," Clint said, wrapping his arms around both her and Andy.

"I'm the lucky one."

"Tomorrow, we'll make plans." His hand groped for hers and, finding it, tucked it against his chest. "Today, we celebrate."

Plans.

She hadn't realized what a beautiful word that was. A future. A future that included Clint. She knew he'd be looking for another job. If he couldn't find one in Last Stop, they'd move. She could work anywhere. As long as they were together, it didn't matter where they lived.

She pulled back the curtains and gasped in pleasure at the strips of color arcing over the mountains. The rainbow, which had eluded her in the past, now beckoned to her, its enticing colors finally within reach. She had only to reach out. . . .

"Look," she said.

With Andy on his shoulder, Clint joined her at the window.

With Clint at her side, she felt she could almost touch it. They would reach for it together.

Together.

"I love you," she whispered.

Chapter Nine

It was a fluke. Ordinarily, she'd never have seen a Denver newspaper. But today a student brought in a copy of the *Denver Post*, folded to an article about the Colorado Rockies. "See, Miss Howard? They're playing next week."

Brittany smiled. A few months ago, Joey McCall had never read a word in his life. Now he was reading, albeit slowly, everything he could lay his hands on. Sports were his particular interest, and he devoured books about sports heroes.

She ruffled his hair. "That's great, Joey. Are you going to see them?"

"My dad's taking me," he said proudly. "See ya," he called over his shoulder as he waved good-bye.

She was still smiling as she flipped through the pa-

132

per, searching for the "Dear Abby" column. A headline in the business section snagged her attention. "Denver-based construction firm wins bid on hospital." She skimmed the article, her mind elsewhere until she saw his name. "Clint Bradley, president and owner, announces Bradley Construction will break ground for hospital next week."

A picture of Clint Bradley followed. Only it wasn't the Clint she knew. This Clint was dressed in evening clothes, with a beautiful woman beside him.

It was a mistake. Maybe there was another Clint Bradley who lived in Denver and looked just like *her* Clint. After all, hadn't she read that everyone had a twin somewhere? She'd show him the picture, and they'd laugh over the coincidence.

She glanced at the picture again and felt the first prick of fear. It wasn't him. It couldn't be. Clint would have told her who he was. He wouldn't deceive her in letting her believe him to be an out-of-work handyman when he owned one of the largest construction firms in the state. He loved her.

For a moment, she allowed herself to believe it wasn't Clint, but another study of the picture told her differently. Even the grainy photo in the newspaper couldn't hide the slash of his cheekbones, the strength of his jaw. She crumpled the paper in her hand, then carefully smoothed it out again.

She read the caption underneath the picture. "Clinton Bradley with fashion designer fianceé, Sherry

King.'' The woman was everything Brittany was not: poised, sophisticated, elegant.

She managed to make it through the rest of the day without falling apart. She drove home by rote, grateful she didn't need to think about what she was doing. Even now, she could feel the layers surrounding her heart freezing over.

Clint was stretching new screen across the front windows. ''You're home early,'' he said, putting down his tools and crossing the room to her.

She avoided his kiss and laid the paper, folded to his picture, down in front of him. ''Is this you?''

Clint looked at it, skimmed the accompanying article, and then turned bleak eyes to her.

If she had any doubt, she knew then. ''It is, isn't it?''

''Yes, it's me.'' His voice was cold, flat.

''Why?''

''Why what?''

''Why did you lie? Why didn't you tell me who you were?''

''I did. I told you my name up front.''

''But you told me you were a handyman.''

''No, *you* told me that,'' he reminded her. ''You even offered me a job.''

''Because I thought you needed it. I thought you were down on your luck.'' She choked back a sob. ''You must have laughed yourself silly over that one. The great Clinton Bradley, working as a handyman.''

''I never laughed at you, Brittany. Never.''

"I even offered to sew up your shirt, patch your jeans. I'll bet you never wore patched jeans in your life."

"You'd lose. How do you think I started out? By owning a company? Sorry to disappoint you. I worked twelve hours a day, seven days a week, turning a two-bit outfit into Bradley Construction. There were years when I never even bought a new shirt. I had patches on my patches. Every cent I made, I put back into the business."

"Then why didn't you tell me?" she asked quietly. "Were you afraid I'd make a play for you because of your money?"

"No. I knew you weren't like that from the start."

"Then, why?"

"I didn't think it mattered at first. And then . . ." He shrugged. "Does it matter that I'm Clint Bradley, company owner, instead of Clint Bradley, handyman?"

"It matters. Not because of what you do, but because you lied to me."

He tried to take her hand, but she yanked it away. "I never meant to hurt you, Brittany."

"You did hurt me. And Andy. You insinuated yourself into our lives. You made me—us—care about you, and then you betrayed us."

"If you'd listen, maybe you'd understand."

"What's to understand? Rich man goes slumming?" The look in his eyes convinced her she'd gone too far, but she didn't care.

"It wasn't like that."

"Then tell me, what was it like?"

"One night, I was going over some contracts when I realized that's all I did anymore. I made money, sure. More money than I ever dreamed existed. But I'd lost something along the way. I decided I had to get away, get back to what I was before Bradley Construction took over my life."

She gestured to the paper. "It says here you won the bid on the hospital."

"Yeah."

"You don't look very happy about it."

"Naturally I'm glad our bid was accepted." But his voice lacked enthusiasm.

"What's the matter? Doesn't making money interest you any more?"

"I'm not going to apologize for what I am," he said coldly. "I'm good at what I do, and I take pride in my work." His voice softened. "But none of it matters if it means I've lost you. I love you, Brittany. Whatever else you think, you've got to believe me."

She couldn't help the warmth that settled around her heart at his words. But it didn't change what he'd done. He'd lied to her. If it'd been anything else, but it hadn't. He'd lied. Even knowing how she felt about dishonesty, he'd kept on lying. "When we started . . . feeling things for each other, why didn't you tell me the truth then?"

"I was afraid."

"Afraid?"

"Of losing you." He watched for her reaction, but her eyes remained carefully blank. "I thought maybe when the time was right . . . but it never was."

"So instead you kept on lying."

"Yeah," he said wearily. "I hoped someday you'd understand."

"You were wrong. I'll never understand lying to people you love. And I'll never forgive you."

There was one more thing. She hated herself for asking, but she had to know. "The woman in the picture . . ."

"She was my fiancée. She dumped me a couple of months ago. The picture's an old one. There hasn't been anyone in my life since I met you."

He tried to take her in his arms, but she backed away from him with such pain in her eyes that he gave up. His arms dropped to his sides.

"Please, go," she said, her voice a thread of sound that wrapped its way around his heart. "Just go."

"We can't leave it this way," he protested, taking a step toward her.

"Please."

He sensed that her fragile control was about to snap.

"All right, we'll have it your way for now."

"It's not my way, Clint. It's the way it has to be. Without honesty, there's nothing."

The bitterness in her voice twisted his heart inside out.

"I'm going now. But I'm coming back, Brittany. And when I do, you're going to listen to me." He speared her with one last look.

"You made a promise once," he said. "I wonder if you'll keep it."

He made himself walk away from her. *One foot in front of the other. That's it, Bradley. You can do it. Don't look back. You're lost if you do, man. Keep your mind on what's important—one step and then another. Pretty soon you'll be out the door.*

He was grateful that traffic on the interstate was heavy, requiring his concentration. If he didn't have the opportunity to think, maybe he'd make it.

Once back in Denver, he headed straight to the office. A consultation with Charlie confirmed what Clint already knew: Bradley Construction had managed just fine without him. Nevertheless, he threw himself into work, clearing his desk of all letters, proposals, and contracts. His secretary gave him wide berth. He didn't blame her.

When he could avoid it no longer, he drove to the house. He walked through the empty rooms, the shrouded furniture resembling misshapen ghosts.

Brittany's small house was more of a home than this brick and concrete monstrosity had ever been. He'd give her time. But after that, he was going after her. And Andy. They belonged to him, whether she admitted it or not.

*   *   *

The door closed, and with it, her heart. Brittany made it to the bathroom and was violently sick. At least he hadn't witnessed that particular humiliation.

She leaned against the bathroom door and sighed. What a fool she'd been. After a lifetime of being cautious, she'd all but invited him into her life. Color scalded her cheeks as she remembered the words of love she'd whispered to him.

Brittany didn't stir from the house for the rest of the day. She felt as though a part of her had died. Even the physical effort required to eat seemed too much, and she picked at the meat loaf she'd prepared for herself and Andy.

Almost as hard as dealing with her own feelings was explaining to Andy. Calling herself all kinds of coward, she shrank from explaining that Clint wouldn't be back; instead, she said he had work in another part of the state.

She caught Andy staring at her oddly and knew he was worried. For his sake, she tried to smile, and carried through with the bedtime ritual of a story and prayers. She must have succeeded, for Andy went to bed looking slightly happier.

One step at a time was her motto for the next week. And if she couldn't manage a whole step, it would be a half step. But, either way, she was going to make it. She was a survivor. She'd proved that before. She'd do it again.

She had to keep busy. If she didn't, she might let herself start to feel.

She half hoped, half dreaded to hear from Clint. But there was no word from him. *And that's the way I want it*, she told herself. It was cold comfort, though, in the lonely days that followed.

The days ran together until she could no longer tell where one stopped and the next began. The nights were the hardest. She imagined Clint's arms around her, holding her. Every word, every syllable of their conversations replayed in her mind until they became a litany of torment, teasing her with the closeness she and Clint had shared and would never share again.

How could he have betrayed me? How could I have been so wrong? The question plagued her nights, feeding her doubts until she wasn't sure what was real any more.

After a few days of self-pity, she took a long look at herself, inside and out. The image in the mirror caused her to wince. Smudges under her eyes had become deep shadows; limp hair framed a face so thin it appeared haggard and old.

The next morning found her dry-eyed and, if not happy, at least accepting. She'd learned a long time ago you couldn't change what life dealt you, only how you reacted. She would not give in to the grief that threatened to engulf her.

She would not let this destroy her.

Time heals all things. Clint repeated the cliche so often that he wondered if sheer repetition could make it true.

He stared into the mirror, revolted by the bleary face that stared back at him. Two days' growth of whiskers, a lack of sleep, and too much black coffee had taken their toll. He felt punchy with exhaustion and cursed the weakness that barely permitted him to stagger from the bathroom back into the bedroom.

The rumpled bedclothes gave mute evidence of his sleepless nights. Empty coffee cups littered the floor, and he glared at them. No amount of caffeine was going to wipe away the guilt that clung to him like a second skin.

He slammed his fist into his palm, remembering the scene in Brittany's house three days ago.

The pain on her face when he'd left her twisted his gut until his whole body throbbed. Her disbelief, turned to anger, then hurt, had imprinted itself on his mind forever. How could he have done it? The question was etched on her face as clearly as if she'd asked the words aloud.

How could he have done it? He asked himself the same question right now, and the answer sickened him. He'd been afraid. Afraid of her reaction when he told her the truth.

Could he ever convince her that he'd stayed because he loved her? That he loved her more than life itself?

He doubted it. How could he expect her to believe him when he'd lied to her from the beginning?

"Enough," he shouted, as though sheer volume could erase the self-pity that engulfed him.

He peeled off his clothes and threw them into the

corner. Stepping into the shower, he turned on the water as hot as he could stand it. He then followed it with a biting cold blast, the spray stinging his body like pellets. He shaved off the stubble of beard.

He dressed quickly, pulling on corduroy slacks and a fisherman knit pullover. A call to an employment agency secured the services of a maid. Ruefully, he glanced about the house and decided he'd need to pay double time for cleaning up the mess he'd created.

He looked—really looked—at his surroundings. His gaze encountered a profusion of chrome and smoked glass, abstract prints and artificial plants. It was elegant, tasteful, and . . . sterile. Brittany would hate it. He'd felt more at home in her small house than he ever had here.

Because work was the only thing that would keep him sane, he headed to the construction site of the new hospital. He donned a hard hat and searched out Charlie.

"Hey, Boss, good to see you," Charlie said, laying a beefy hand on Clint's shoulder.

"Everything all right here?" Clint asked.

"Smooth as silk. Why don't you take some time off?" Charlie suggested. "You look like you've just been run over by a Mack truck."

"Thanks," Clint said dryly. "You sure know how to cheer a man up."

"I didn't mean nothin' by it."

"I know." Clint managed a weak smile and headed

back to his car. "I'll be at the office if something should come up."

"Sure, Boss."

The usual assortment of memos, contracts, and project summaries littered his desk. For once, Clint didn't duck the paperwork, but welcomed it as a distraction from his thoughts. But work didn't prove the remedy it had in the past.

The idea that had been simmering in the back of his mind began to take shape.

A call to a friend on the Board of Education confirmed what Brittany had told him about the need for a support organization for families of special-needs children. Several such centers existed in Denver, but none in the area surrounding Last Stop.

"Boss, you sure about this?" Charlie Owens asked when Clint approached him about taking over Bradley Construction on a full-time basis.

"I'm sure, Charlie," Clint said. "Real sure. For the first time in a long time, I'm doing what I want to do."

With Charlie as manager of Bradley Construction, Clint knew the business would be in capable hands. Now he was free to concentrate on the Rainbow Children's Center.

The sense of purpose that had been missing from his life returned. His excitement grew as he made plans. He'd design and build the center himself.

He smiled, thinking that Brittany would like the name. Abruptly, his smile faded. As always, thoughts of Brittany had the power to twist him inside out.

He longed for some kind of news of her and Andy. Remembering the letter he'd seen about Andy's operation, he looked up the doctor's name in the phone book and placed a call.

"We cannot give out that kind of information over the phone," a woman's voice repeated patiently over the line.

"All I want is a word with Dr. Jeffers," Clint said, keeping a tight rein on his temper.

"I'm sorry, but the doctor is in conference," the same bored voice said.

"Then, make an appointment for me," he told her. He bit out the necessary information and hung up.

What good it would do to talk with Andy's doctor, he wasn't sure. All he knew was that he needed some kind of link to Brittany.

Two days later Clint paced impatiently in the waiting room. "Mr. Bradley, the doctor will be with you as soon as he can," the receptionist told him, a reproving frown on her face.

"Thanks." He forced himself to sit down and pick up a magazine. After five minutes, he slammed it down on the table. He'd been looking at it upside down and hadn't noticed until now.

"Mr. Bradley, if you'll follow me." The receptionist led him to a consulting room.

After a short wait, the doctor appeared. "What can I do for you, Mr. Bradley?" He consulted his clipboard. "I see here you're suffering from excruciating headaches."

"I lied, Dr. Jeffers," Clint said bluntly. "I want to know what's going on with Brittany Howard and Andy."

The doctor laid down the clipboard and stood. "You look like an intelligent man, Mr. Bradley. You ought to know I can't give out that kind of information."

"If you won't tell me, I'll find it out some other way." Clint clenched and unclenched his fists.

Dr. Jeffers sat down. "Why don't you simply ask Ms. Howard?"

"I can't," Clint admitted. "She won't speak to me."

The doctor checked his watch. "I've scheduled an hour for your appointment. Maybe you'd better tell me the whole thing."

Slowly, Clint divulged his story. He didn't spare himself in the telling, but told the doctor everything, including his own deception.

"And now she refuses to see you?" Dr. Jeffers zeroed in on the most important point.

Clint nodded. "Not that I blame her. Right now, though, I'm concerned about Andy. Does Brittany have enough money to pay for an operation?"

Dr. Jeffers didn't answer immediately. He wrote a figure on a sheet of paper and passed it to Clint, who gave a low whistle.

"That's only the hospital charge. I'm waiving my fee, but . . . "

Clint nodded and then stood. "Thank you, Doctor. I promise you won't regret this."

He didn't delude himself into thinking Brittany would thank him for what he was about to do. She was as independent as they come. He liked her the better for it. But, this once, he intended to ignore it.

He didn't stop to change clothes. During the three-hour drive, he went through a dozen scenarios of what he would say to Brittany. But the only one that made sense, the only one he wanted to say, was "I love you."

His first reaction upon seeing the white clapboard house was that he'd come home. The second was pride. He'd made a difference here. The porch no longer sagged, the house gleamed with its fresh coat of paint. Yes, he'd made a difference.

He pounded at the door, nervousness making him louder than he intended.

Within a few seconds, Brittany appeared.

"I have to talk with you."

She attempted to slam the door, but his foot blocked her efforts. He edged his way inside and shut the door behind him. Now, leaning against it, he studied her and frowned.

"You've lost weight." He touched a hand to her cheek and let it fall to her neck, tracing her delicate collar bone.

"No. Maybe. I don't know. It doesn't matter."

"It matters."

He continued to trail his fingers along her shoulder, dropping them to her arm, and felt her tremble.

"Go away, Clint. We have nothing to say to each other."

"We have everything to say. And sooner or later, you'll admit it. But right now, we have to talk about Andy."

"Leave Andy out of this. Isn't it enough you made him care for you and then left him? You were the first man he's been close to in two years. What do you think it did to him when he found out you didn't care about him at all?"

"Did you tell him that?"

She shook her head. "I couldn't. I told him you had to go away."

"I didn't have to go away," he said quietly.

"And what was I suppose to do? Just pretend nothing happened? That you hadn't lied to me? To us?" She sank down wearily on a chair. "Say what you have to say."

"What are you going to do about Andy's operation?"

"I don't know," she whispered.

"This isn't the time for beating about the bush. Do you have the money?"

She looked at her hands. "If I decide to go ahead with the operation, I'll get the money. You don't have to concern yourself about it."

"Where?"

"As I said, that's none of your concern. What I decide is between Andy and me."

"Can't you believe I want to help you? I'll give you the money."

She flinched as though he'd struck her.

He winced at the look of pain that crossed her face. "All right, call it a loan. Call it whatever you want. Please, just let me help."

"Andy'll be home soon. Please . . . leave. Seeing you again would—"

"I'll be back. I promised Andy a fishing trip. And I don't break my promises."

No, only hearts, she thought. And that's even worse.

"Aunt Brittany, what happened to Clint?" Andy asked after school. "Why's he staying away for so long? Why hasn't he come back yet?"

"Clint had to go back to his old job."

"But he'll be back, won't he?"

"I don't think so."

"But he promised he'd take me fishing. Clint said it's very important to keep your promises and to never, never break them."

Brittany pulled Andy onto her lap. "Sometimes, it's not possible to keep a promise. Sometimes, even though a person may want to keep his promise very much, he just can't."

"But Clint said—"

"Andy, Clint cares for you very much. But he has a life of his own. One that doesn't include us." She brushed a stray curl back from his forehead. "He had to go back to his old life."

"Back where?"

"To his home, his work. Just like I have work here and you go to school here, Clint has work he has to do."

Andy's lip trembled. "You mean he might never come back? Ever?"

She chose her words carefully. "Probably not, sweetheart. We always knew Clint couldn't stay with us forever, didn't we?" When he didn't answer, she said, "Clint had things he had to do. A job that took him away."

"But his job was here," Andy said. "He fixed things around here. Wasn't that a job? He told me I was his number one helper. I couldn't be a helper if he didn't have a job, could I?"

How could she argue with a six-year-old's logic?

"Andy, sometimes grown-ups can have two jobs. When Clint came to us, he already had another job. He stayed with us until . . . until he had to go back to his other job." How could a child possibly understand such a garbled explanation? She didn't understand it herself.

"Are you mad at Clint?"

"Mad? Why do you ask that?"

"Because you look sad all the time. Was Clint mean to you?"

He doesn't know what he's saying, Brittany reminded herself as a fresh wave of pain swept over her.

"No, honey, he wasn't mean to me. Clint would never hurt me." As she said the words, she knew they were true. Clint would never hurt her. How had she ever thought otherwise? Tears stung her eyes at the realization.

"I don't like Clint anymore," Andy startled her by saying. "He made you cry. I never want to see him again. I hope he never comes back."

Tears streamed down his face, and his shoulders quivered from sobs.

Brittany gathered him to her, understanding he was only lashing out as she had earlier. "It's all right," she crooned. "It's all right."

"I hate him," Andy said, breaking away from her. "I wish he'd never come here."

"You don't really mean that. Sometimes when we're hurting, we say things we don't mean."

Andy looked up at her. "Do you ever do that?"

"I'm afraid so." Squeezing his hand, she prayed her voice wouldn't break. She couldn't let Andy see how vulnerable she was. She had to be strong for him and tried to put a smile in her voice. "But we have each other. Just like always."

"Yeah, I know." He slid down off her lap. "Is it all right if I go lie down?"

"Now?" Andy never wanted to nap during the day. He'd told her often enough that naps were for babies.

"I'm sort of tired." He trudged off to the bedroom, his limp more pronounced than usual, dejection written in every line of his slight body.

Ironically, in trying to make Andy understand, she had begun to understand also. Fresh tears trickled down her cheeks as she realized how Clint must be feeling.

How he must hate her for the horrible things she'd said to him.

She shook her head. In letting go of the pain, she experienced a cleansing of her spirit that had been too long in coming. Hatred cankered the soul, she realized, souring everything with its acid. She wouldn't let it fester inside of her any more.

In learning to forgive, she faced the most difficult hurdle yet—forgiving herself. Things she thought she'd buried now surfaced, and she confronted them with ruthless self-examination: things like not being perfect, expecting everyone whom she loved to be perfect; things like understanding why her parents had tried to protect Andy with their lies.

Maybe it wasn't too late for everything. Before she could talk herself out of it, she picked up the phone and punched out the number she hadn't been able to forget.

"Mom, it's Brittany."

She waited while her mother cried and then called her father. "Dad, it's Brittany."

The tears flowed, but with them came a tentative stab at a new beginning.

"I'll let you know about the operation," she said. Before she severed the connection, she whispered, "I love you."

Her parents' words were lost as she gently replaced the phone. She wasn't ready to hear their reply yet. Her own words had surprised her, probably more than they had her parents. She needed time to accept her feelings. Maybe someday they could forgive each other for being human.

This first step toward rebuilding her relationship with her parents lightened her heart. She wrote a long letter to them, enclosing pictures of Andy. But it didn't stop the ache of losing Clint.

Loneliness loomed ahead of her as a frightening specter. The idea of falling in love again was unthinkable, for she knew she'd never feel this way about another man.

Scenes unfurled before her in slow motion, their colors a muted sepia. Clint painting the fence, Clint washing dishes and spraying her with soap bubbles, Clint scrambling eggs for their breakfast. Other pictures came unbidden with the onslaught of a dam breaking: the two of them having a water fight, going to the auction together, wallpapering her bedroom.

Each took on a life of its own as it unfolded in her mind. She wanted to reach out, to freeze a frame, and hold it in her hand, for that was all she had left of him—memories of a man who would always possess her heart.

Clint. Was it all me? Did you feel it too?

Slowly, she started the process of living all over again. She had done it before, and she would do it now. If she had little heart for new beginnings, she would find it eventually.

Her life revolved around Andy and her students. Without them, she was sure she would go quietly mad. Her job, caring for Andy, fixing up the house, filled the hours. Only the nights were empty, the lonely hours stretching into eternity, the silence heavy with memories.

After agonizing over the decision about Andy's operation, she decided to approach him about it. She couldn't postpone it any longer.

"Andy, you remember we talked once about going back to the hospital someday."

A wary look crept into his eyes.

"Dr. Jeffers thinks he has an operation that can help you walk without braces."

"You promised I wouldn't have to go there again."

"I know. But if there's a chance, any chance at all, I think we have to take it." She didn't tell him what else the doctor had said. She couldn't.

"You promised," he said once more.

"I wish there was another way, but there isn't. I trust Dr. Jeffers. If he says he can do this, I believe him." She waited.

"Would I really walk without these?" he asked, pointing to the metal and leather braces that encased his legs.

"I think so."

"Do you want me to have this operation, Aunt Brittany?"

The hardest question of all. "Yes. I do."

"Okay. If you say so, then I'll do it."

She held him close, humbled by his trust in her.

With a feeling of hope mingled with a large dose of anxiety, she wrote Dr. Jeffers, asking him to schedule the operation as soon as possible. Though it would mean Andy's missing the next semester of school, she feared she might get cold feet if she postponed it.

A letter from Dr. Jeffers two days later spun her plans into a tail wind. She scanned the letter and gasped. Even with his fee waived, the projected bill was out of her reach.

She stared at it once more. The figures hadn't changed. How could she possibly come up with ten thousand dollars? Even if she sold everything they had and emptied her checking account, she'd have nowhere near that amount. She considered asking her parents and knew she couldn't. Their savings had been stretched to the limit during the last few years since her father's heart attack.

She struggled with trying to find a solution. When the letter bearing Dr. Jeffers's business address came two days later, she opened it, expecting to find his regrets that he wouldn't be able to perform the operation. She scanned its contents, then read it through again. Andy's operation would be funded through an anonymous source for "research purposes."

She could scarcely believe it. Now she had only to pack what they'd need, close up the house, and resign from her job. That gave her a momentary pang. She loved what she did. Moreover, she loved her students. But it wouldn't be forever. She and Andy would be coming back.

The preparations to leave were accomplished in less time then she had believed possible. Ralph had been delivered to Jim, who had offered to keep him until they returned. She had cancelled the newspaper and milk delivery.

Only packing remained. Funny how the smallest thing could cause the tears to surface. Folding the quilt she and Clint had bought at the auction . . . wrapping tissue paper around the prism mobile with its rainbow of colors . . . storing the ice cream maker in its box.

She shook away the memories. Finally, accepting the inevitable, she let them have their way. Pain couldn't last forever. Could it?

A week later, she gazed at the house, now closed up, window shades drawn, door bolted. Thanks to Clint, the porch railing now stood proudly erect, the once-dingy fence sparkling white under its coat of paint. She smiled, remembering the day she and Clint had painted the fence. They had a water fight and . . .

She'd thought she had no more tears left and swiped at them angrily. Minutes later, when the tears came again, she didn't brush them away.

Chapter Ten

"**I** wish it could be me instead of Andy."

Dr. Jeffers pressed her hand. "It would be easier on all of us if we could take away a child's pain. Unfortunately, even with all our advances, we haven't figured out a way to do that."

"I'm just having a case of nerves. The person who's paying for the operation—I'd like to thank him. Do you think I could meet him sometime?"

Dr. Jeffers was at once briskly professional. "I'm afraid not. He prefers to remain anonymous." The doctor stood, signaling that the interview was over.

"I see. Thank you," she said and quietly closed the door behind her.

She found Andy in the brightly colored play room that Dr. Jeffers reserved for his young patients.

"Andy, time to go."

"Aw, Aunt Brittany," he protested, awkwardly getting to his feet. "Do we have to? I was just about to make a bridge." He gestured to a pile of interlocking blocks, a splash of color against the muted carpet.

" 'Fraid so. We'll come back another time and you can finish your bridge."

They stopped at the ice cream parlor located in the lobby of the hospital and splurged on a treat. Andy's eyes widened as he struggled with the difficult choice of deciding between a banana split and a chocolate malt.

As he devoured the chocolate malt, Brittany sipped at her lemonade. A slight frown creased her forehead and she pressed her fingers to her temples as though she could wipe away the worry with the simple action.

In an effort to take her mind off the operation, she glanced about at the other patrons. Two mischievous boys, obviously identical twins, scampered around their mother as she tried to balance a baby in her arms and hold three dripping ice cream cones.

With a quick "I'll be right back" to Andy, she approached the harassed young mother. "May I?" she asked and held out her hands.

An assessing look was followed by a nod of relief. "Please." The woman relinquished the baby gratefully and paid for her cones.

Brittany placed the baby on her hip in time-honored fashion and shepherded the boys to a small table. She unfolded paper napkins and tucked them into the boys' shirts. "There. Now, you two big boys need to help your mother. I know she depends on you," she said in a conspiratorial whisper. "Because your little sister can't help much, can she?"

A look passed between the two boys, and they nodded.

"Thank you so much," their mother said as she handed out the ice cream cones. "I don't know how I'd have managed without your help."

"I enjoyed it," Brittany assured her. "You have beautiful children."

The young woman smiled fondly. "They are that. They're also a handful. I don't know what made me think we could stop in here without it turning into a major production."

"How old are your boys?"

"Five." The woman glanced at Andy. "Your little boy looks about the same age."

"He turned six last summer. I guess we'd better be on our way." Before leaving, she turned to give the boys a just-between-us-look. "Remember what we talked about?"

They nodded solemnly, and she winked at them.

"Thanks again." The young mother waved goodbye while balancing her baby on her hip.

Brittany sketched a wave and helped Andy take their cups to the trash can, a sadness in her eyes.

"Let's do that again," he said as they left the building.

"I think we can arrange that," she promised, shaking off her depression. They took a taxi back to the hotel where they had taken a room.

Andy bounced on the bed. "I like it here. This bed must be ten feet off the ground."

She laughed. "Not quite, but I'm glad you like it. Do you want to go out tonight or shall we splurge and order room service?"

"Can we? Will they bring the food right to us?"

"Right to our door. You can order anything you want," she said. "Think of this as an adventure."

"An adventure?" Andy's eyes widened. "Then I want a hamburger, fries, and milk shake."

She wondered what the hotel's chef would think of such an order. "We'll make it two."

Later, after she'd tucked Andy into bed, she turned on the TV and sank down on a chair. As she stared unseeingly at the screen, a sadness settled around her heart. The image of the young mother and her children wouldn't leave Brittany's mind. Despite her harried look, the woman had appeared happy with her little brood.

At last Brittany admitted the cause of her dejection. She would never experience the loving havoc of raising a large family, as she'd once dreamed. And Andy would never know the noise and fun, squabbles and confusion of having brothers and sisters.

As they had so frequently in the last week, thoughts of Clint filtered through her mind. She remembered the conversation she'd had with him about marrying and having children. How sure she'd been then that she didn't need anyone else, that Andy was all she'd ever need. She cringed now, realizing how arrogant she must have sounded.

A tiny sob escaped as she acknowledged how much she missed Clint. She'd ordered him out of her life. She'd thought the pain would go away. It had eventually subsided to a dull ache, for which she was grateful. But the hurt was always there, a constant reminder of what might have been.

Could she spend the rest of her life with it?

"The operation was a success."

The doctor's words reached her through a haze, and she blinked twice, trying to take them in.

"It went . . . well?"

A broad smile creased his face. "Very well. Of course, Andy's going to be in casts for a while. Then we'll start the process of teaching him to walk again. This time without crutches. He's got a whole new set of muscles he needs to learn how to use."

She pressed her fingers to her eyes. The tears seeped through anyway. "Thank you, Doctor. Thank you very much."

"It was my pleasure. Now, I suggest a rest for you. You've been here over six hours."

"But Andy—I want to see him."

Dr. Jeffers led her to the elevator. "Andy won't come out of the sedation for a couple of hours. The best thing you can do for yourself and for him is to get some rest."

"But—"

"You won't do him any good if you collapse the first time he sees you," the doctor reminded her gently. "You're right, of course." Impulsively, she reached up to kiss his cheek. "Thank you for everything."

The cold stung her face as she walked through the automatic doors, but she hardly felt it. A northern wind cut through her with merciless energy. Storm clouds hovered in an ashen sky, a whisper of snow urging the scurrying pedestrians to hurry to their destinations.

Her thin coat, flung hastily over her shoulders, provided scant protection against the biting wind. Still, Brittany walked on, oblivious to everything but the knowledge that Andy was all right. Beside this, nothing else mattered, not even the fact that Clint would never again be a part of their lives.

That wasn't true, she acknowledged in a burst of honesty. Clint would always be a part of her life . . . because she loved him.

The curious looks of others scurrying to escape the freezing rain finally registered, and she gathered her coat about her more tightly. A sudden respite from the storm caused her to look up to find an umbrella sheltering her. Clint was by her side; instinctively, she moved closer to him.

"Come on," he urged. "Let's get out of this before we both catch pneumonia."

Too weary to argue or to question how he'd suddenly appeared, she allowed herself to be guided to a small cafe tucked in between the expensive boutiques which lined the street. Inside, Clint helped her off with her coat and hung it on a nearby rack. Water trickled from it, leaving a small puddle on the wood floor.

Brittany caught a glimpse of her reflection in the window and moaned. Suddenly made aware of her hair plastered to her face, her sodden clothes, and washed-out complexion, she wished she was anywhere else but here.

Clint watched her and guessed what she was thinking. She was too thin, too pale, too tired . . . and he knew he'd never seen a more beautiful sight. Gold hair, shorter now, framed her face with wispy curls. Dark shadows beneath eyes that looked too large for her face gave her a fragile air that made him want to take her in his arms and protect her. And something more. He wanted to cherish her. Always. Forever.

The hidden strength he'd first noticed about her, the steel tempered by fire, was still there in the proud way she held herself, the tilt of her chin, the eyes that said she would not bow to whatever fate chose to hand her. But he'd seen the vulnerability underneath, the softness she tried so hard to conceal.

The subtle fragrance she wore wrapped itself around him, weaving its spell over him as it had in the past. It teased him with memories of when she had wrapped her arms around him and murmured words of love.

Forcibly, he restrained himself from taking her into his arms and kissing her. Instead, he steered her toward the corner booth which the waitress indicated. He waited until she slid into the banquette seat before saying anything.

"I like your hair," he said.

"Thank you."

"Your hair was the first thing I noticed about you." His voice turned husky, and he cleared his throat. "I tried to catch you at the hospital, but the nurse said you'd already left."

She nodded.

He took her hand. "How's Andy doing?"

"Better than we dared hope for. He's still under sedation right now, but his vital signs are good."

"I'm glad."

"The doctor thinks he'll be walking soon, without crutches or braces."

The pressure on her fingers increased. "Andy's a trooper. He'll soon be running circles around us."

He wondered if she understood the significance of the last word. A glance at her confirmed that she did. She would have withdrawn her hand, but he refused to release it.

She looked pointedly at it. "I should be going."

"We haven't ordered yet."

"I'm not very hungry."

His gaze took in the shadows beneath her eyes, the way the skin stretched tautly across her cheekbones, the tired droop of her lips. His fingers circled her wrist easily, and he frowned over her obvious weight loss.

"I'd say you hadn't eaten a decent meal in weeks. You won't be any help to Andy if you make yourself sick.'' He couldn't help the bit of anger that slipped through.

''I know,'' she said quietly. ''I just haven't felt hungry lately.''

The waitress returned, saving him the need to answer. Without consulting Brittany, he ordered tomato soup, salad, and burgers for the two of them.

Her eyes widened at the amount of food that appeared at their table. ''I'm not very hungry.''

''Eat what you can.''

Cautiously, she took a bite of her salad and realized, contrary to her protestations, that she was ravenous for the first time in weeks. Clint didn't try to make conversation, and for that she was grateful.

Fifteen minutes later, she pushed her plate away. ''I guess I was hungrier than I thought.''

''It's no wonder.''

''Clint—''

''Brittany—''

Brown eyes collided with brown. Their gazes caught and held.

Hungrily, Brittany drank in the sight of him, intensely aware of just how much she'd missed him. With his hair darkened by the rain, his chocolate-brown eyes made more magnetic than ever by the tan turtleneck he wore, he was a feast for her eyes.

The love she'd never stopped feeling was there, naked, exposed for all to see. Fortunately, he looked away just then as he scanned the room for the waitress, missing the emotion she could not disguise. Conscious of how much she'd almost given away through a glance, she dropped her gaze just as Clint turned back to her.

She searched for a neutral topic of conversation. "I . . . uh . . . called my parents."

He looked up.

"We talked. They're coming to see Andy tomorrow."

"How do you feel about it?"

"Nervous. Scared. Happy."

He pressed her hand. "I'm glad."

"So am I." She paused, unsure of how to say what needed to be said. But she owed him. And she always paid her debts. "Thank you."

He looked surprised. "For what?"

"You made me see that I was wrong. Maybe they were too. I don't know any more. I don't even care. I just want us to be a family again."

"How long are they staying?"

"I don't know. We're going to play it by ear. If everything goes all right, they might stay for Christmas."

"I should have told you the truth from the beginning."

"Why didn't you?"

"Because I was afraid. Afraid you'd send me away. Some excuse, isn't it? I served three years in 'Nam, have a dozen medals for bravery, and I'm a fraud."

"Don't say that." She couldn't bear to hear the self-condemnation in his voice.

"It's true." When she would have protested again, he held up a hand. "Don't get me wrong. I wanted to tell you. A thousand times, I tried. Only the timing never seem right."

Brittany blinked back the tears. "What happened, happened. We can't change it. Only go on from there."

"If you really mean that . . ." He tilted her chin up, saw the tears shimmering in her eyes. He brushed a gentle finger across her cheek. "I want us to begin again. Can you forgive me?"

"I already have," she said, her voice husky with unshed tears.

He expelled a deep breath. "You once said you loved me. Is that still true?"

"Why?" She held her breath.

"Because I want to marry you."

A spark of hope shone in her eyes but dulled as he said, "I want to take care of you and Andy—if you'll let me."

A spasm of pain crossed her face at his words, words she felt were inspired by guilt and a strong streak of pity. She put a hand to her mouth, trying to control the trembling of her lips. "I don't think we can." Her voice held a wealth of sadness. *Clint deserved a woman whom he could love, not one he felt tied to by guilt, or worse, pity.*

"Won't you give us a chance? Pretend we've met for the first time today." He brought her hand to his mouth, his lips replacing his fingers as he pressed a kiss to the sensitive skin of the inside of her wrist.

Her determination almost faltered at his touch. "That's just it. We'd be pretending. We can't turn back the clock."

Clint reached out to brush her cheek when, abruptly, she stood.

"It was good seeing you."

He jumped up. "Brittany, wait . . ."

She walked away without a backward glance. It was the hardest thing she'd ever had to do. She willed her legs to keep moving and tried to ignore the fact that her heart was breaking. If she didn't allow herself to think or feel, she might be able to walk away without disgracing herself.

Clint stared after her bleakly. He'd known all along it was a long shot. One he had little hope of winning. But he had to try, didn't he?

The waitress appeared with the bill. He slapped down a couple of bills on the table and scowled so fiercely at her that she cringed.

"Sorry," he muttered and laid down another bill.

Outside, sleet stung his face with a thousand pinpricks of cold. He squinted against the blur, hoping he'd see which way Brittany had gone. Snow clung to his eyelashes and brows, silvering them with delicate flakes. Cold numbed his face and hands, turned his feet to stumps of ice. If only it could deaden the ache in his heart as well.

Blindly, he walked back to his hotel, impervious to the wind lashing his face. The demon *if* tormented his thoughts, torturing his soul with might-have-beens.

If he'd given in to his first impulse, which was to take Brittany in his arms and kiss her . . . If he hadn't stayed away from her for so long, thinking she needed time . . . If he'd forced her to listen . . . He'd have *made* her see how much he wanted her, how much he needed her. How much he loved her.

Back at her hotel room, Brittany put a quivering hand to her lips. She'd walked away from Clint when all she'd wanted to do was to hurl herself in his arms and pretend that the last ten weeks had never happened.

It would have taken one small word from her to have all she ever wanted. Why couldn't she just this once take what life was offering? If she'd said yes, Clint would be hers. She would have a husband and Andy a father. They'd have more children. Clint would make a good father. Then why didn't she?

She knew the answer—she just didn't want to face it. Now, her innate honesty forced her to admit the truth. She wanted to be loved. Never once during his proposal had he mentioned the words. He'd told her he wanted to *take care* of her and Andy. It was a far cry from love. Too far for her to accept.

Perhaps if she'd told him how she felt . . . she rejected the idea immediately. He'd have felt even *more* bound to her, bound by his own scruples and sense of honor. She didn't want that. Love freed; it didn't chain. If she accepted his proposal, they would both regret it. She wouldn't—couldn't—do that to him.

She loved him too much.

Chapter Eleven

Clint holed up in his office for the next two days, burying himself in work. The Rainbow Children's Center was progressing faster than he had dared to hope. Everything was perfect, or it would have been, had Brittany been there to share it with him. He'd wanted to tell her of the Rainbow Children's Center, but he wouldn't use it to pressure her. As much as he wanted her love, he wouldn't buy it.

On the third day, and several gallons of coffee later, he gave himself the tongue-lashing he deserved and ventured out. He'd put off the visit too long already.

Outside, he ignored his car and decided to walk. The plastic Santas who decked the street signs mocked his mood. Not until he saw a small boy, nose pressed against a store window, did he stop. A display of electric trains and stuffed animals drew his interest. He walked into the toy store. Twenty minutes later, he left, well pleased with his purchases.

The pungent aroma of antiseptic coupled with the overpowering fragrance of too many flowers gave hospitals a distinctive scent all their own, Clint decided as he inquired at the front desk which room Andy occupied.

He carried a huge stuffed elephant, its floppy ears and silly grin nudging smiles from harried nurses and preoccupied doctors. Tucked under his other arm was a hand-held video game.

Doubts pestered him, and he questioned if he should even be here as he shouldered the door open.

"Clint, you came."

Andy's scream of delight wiped away all his uncertainty.

"Sure I came, partner," he said, crossing the room. He bent to ruffle sleep-mussed hair and brush a kiss on Andy's cheek. "Did you think I'd stay away?"

"I knew you'd come. Aunt Brittany said not to hope too much, but I knew."

The simple faith touched Clint. *Why hadn't he come sooner?*

Pride had a lot to answer for. He swallowed hard. "I made a promise, didn't I? When you're well enough and the weather's better, we'll go fishing. Just you and me. How 'bout it?"

"Great. Remember the time you and me and Aunt

Brittany went fishing? And we caught those humongous ones? And—''

Pictures filled his mind. Pictures of Brittany. Her hair pulled back into a pony tail, her nose shiny, her jeans rolled up above her knees. Suddenly, a different picture took its place: Brittany, her lips parted, her eyes soft and dreamy.

"Yeah, I remember."

A thin hand shook his arm. "Hey, Clint, what's the matter? You sound sort of funny."

"Nothing's the matter, partner. Nothing at all." He pulled himself out of the past and focused on the small boy beside him. "Your aunt and Dr. Jeffers tell me you're going to be up and walking before we know it."

Now it was Andy who withdrew. "Yeah. Maybe." His shoulders sagged; his lips curved downward in a noticeable droop.

Clint frowned. "What's the matter? I thought you'd be excited."

"I'm afraid," Andy whispered.

"Afraid of what?"

"That I won't be able to walk as well as they say. And then everyone is going to be real disappointed. Maybe even mad at me."

Awkwardly, Clint put an arm about Andy, not an easy task when the little boy was surrounded by tubes, monitors, and other gadgets. "Do you really think your aunt would be mad at you?"

Andy hung his head. "No. Not really. But she'll cry. I don't like to see her cry."

Neither do I. "I know. Most of us don't like to see people we love hurting. But hurting is part of life. If we didn't hurt sometimes, it'd mean we didn't care. And that's the most awful feeling in the whole world."

Andy looked up at him. "How do you know?"

"Because I've been there. And it's lonely. Your aunt loves you more than anything in the world. She'd never get mad at you for something you can't control." Gently, he pulled Andy closer. "But I have a feeling you're going to walk. Walk and run and do everything you want to."

"Even play baseball?"

"Even play baseball."

Andy's small hand curved around Clint's larger one. "I'm glad you came."

"Me too."

Andy shifted in the bed, straining to look up at the large man beside him. "Why did you go away? I thought you liked Aunt Brittany and me. I thought you wanted to marry us."

Clint kept holding the hand nestled in his own even though he felt a jolt at Andy's words. "I wanted to. More than I can tell you. But sometimes grown-ups have problems they can't work out."

"Did you and Aunt Brittany have pr . . . problems?"

"I'm afraid so."

"She cried all the time after you left. She said she had a cold, but I knew it was because of you." Andy fixed Clint with an accusing look. "Why did you make her cry?"

"I didn't want to. Do you believe that?" As Andy nodded, Clint said, "Sometimes adults hurt each other without meaning to. I would never hurt her on purpose."

"Does that make it okay? That you didn't hurt her on purpose, I mean?"

"No," Clint said, the hitch in his voice a reminder of what might have been. "It doesn't make it all right."

A fresh dose of guilt sluiced over him, guilt caused by the innocent words of a six-year-old. How did you tell a small boy that love didn't always win out, that sometimes hurt and pain were the victors in a world that was too often neither black nor white, but murky shades of gray?

Andy tugged at Clint's sleeve. "But people who love each other live in the same house. Don't you *love* us?"

"I love you," Clint said, his voice sandpaper-rough as he tried to keep the tears at bay. "I love you and your aunt. Even if I can't be your dad, I'll always love you. Nothing can change that."

Andy's lips quivered. "Did I make you mad? One of my friends at school said her daddy left her mom and her because she left her bike in the driveway."

Clint squeezed the slight body close to his own hard one. "No, champ. You didn't make me mad."

The crisp rustling of a starched uniform announced the presence of the nurse. "Mr. Bradley, I'm afraid you'll have to leave now. Andy needs his rest."

Andy clung to his hand. "Will you come back, Clint? Please."

"You bet. Just try to keep me away." He ruffled the strawberry-blond hair once more.

"Promise?"

"Promise."

Outside in the corridor, Clint waited for the nurse. When she reappeared, he stopped her. "Where can I find Dr. Jeffers?"

She gave him an appraising look before answering. "At this hour, he's probably in an office he keeps here in the hospital. In another hour, he'll be making rounds."

"Thanks." He strode down the hallway, found the elevator, and pushed the button for the fourth floor. Within a few minutes, he knocked on the doctor's door.

A harassed voice bade him enter. Dr. Jeffers looked up from a sheaf of papers. "Oh. Bradley. What can I do for you?"

"It's about Andy Howard, Doctor. I wanted to hear from you how he's doing."

The doctor pushed up his glasses and sat back in his chair. "You've seen him, I take it?"

Clint nodded. "Today. The nurse says he's doing well. But—"

"You wanted a second opinion." The doctor laughed at his own joke. "Well, she's right. Nurses usually are, you know. Andy should be walking on his own within four months. While he's here, we'll start physical therapy. In a few weeks, he can go home and come back on an outpatient basis.''

Clint expelled a long breath. "That's great. About the cost—"

"Your check more than covered it."

"But if there's anything more, you'll call me? You still have my number?"

"Yes, yes. You've made that quite clear. What I don't understand is why you don't tell Ms. Howard what you're doing."

Because she'd tell me to go straight to the devil. "She has enough on her mind right now. I don't want to bother her with this."

"Brittany Howard is a very proud woman," the doctor said thoughtfully.

"Yes, she is."

"She might be upset if she learned she'd been deceived."

She'd be furious, Clint interpreted. "Yes, I think she might."

"And you still want to handle things this way?"

"I still want to handle things this way."

The doctor stood.

Clint stood. "Thank you, Doctor. I'll be in touch."

Outside, he inhaled deeply, savoring the antiseptic-free air. The cold wave had chased away the smog that usually hung over the city and blanketed it in a layer of fleecy snow. Ice sheathed the streets, making them treacherous to motorists and pedestrians alike.

He headed to his car, a cautious optimism replacing

the gloom that had encased him during the last few days as he recalled Andy's words.

"Aunt Brittany cried all the time after you left."

Surely that wasn't the behavior of someone who didn't love him. Didn't that imply she cared? Just a little? He dared hope he was right. He didn't think he could bear it if he were wrong this time.

The doorbell chimed. Brittany groaned, not in the mood tonight for carolers. She'd returned from the hospital thirty minutes ago and was just about to change clothes. A talk with Dr. Jeffers had given her a lot to think about.

Pausing, she considered ignoring the bell. Good manners won out. Slipping on a robe, she pasted a smile on her face and answered the door.

Clint stood there, bulky in a sheepskin coat, wool scarf, and boots. "Merry Christmas, Brittany."

"Clint." For the life of her, she couldn't think of anything else to say.

"I hope you don't mind. I have a gift for Andy."

"Of course not." She stepped back, gesturing for him to come in.

He stomped his feet on the mat, shaking off the snow, before handing her a brightly wrapped package. "I love snow. But enough is enough."

"I know what you mean." She looked at him uncertainly. "Can I take your coat?"

"Yes, please." He shrugged out of the sheepskin jacket and handed it to her.

"Would you like some hot chocolate? I have some made. Or maybe some cider?"

He grasped at the chance to prolong the visit and said, "Hot chocolate sounds good."

She gave him a tentative smile. "I'll be back in a minute."

Clint looked around at the small apartment. Dingy brown carpet covered the floor, with an equally dingy sofa providing the only seating. He swore silently because she'd been forced to live in such a place.

"I put marshmallows in it," Brittany said, emerging from the kitchen. "I hope you like them."

"I never drink hot chocolate without them." He didn't mention that the only time he drank hot chocolate was when he was with her.

"Would you like to sit down?" She pointed to the lumpy, vinyl-covered sofa.

"Thanks."

They both perched awkwardly on the edge of the couch. A painful silence stretched between them. Clint knew a moment's sadness at it. There'd been a time when there was no constraint between them.

"Thanks for the present," she said. "Andy loves presents, the more the better."

"I hope he likes it. It's an electric train set."

"I'm sure he will." She winced at how stilted her words sounded and glanced at Clint, wondering if he felt as ill at ease as she did. "Dr. Jeffers told me what you did, paying for Andy's operation. It wasn't his fault," she said when he looked thunderous. "I badgered him until he gave in.'' She looked down at her hands. ''I don't know what to say, except thank you.''

Clint muttered something under his breath. ''I don't want your thanks.''

''I'll pay you back.''

''I don't want your money. I want . . . you know what I want!''

His outburst startled her, causing her to spill the chocolate. The hot liquid scalded her fingers.

Clint took the cup from her, led her into the kitchen, turned on the faucet, and held her hand under the cold water. The stinging in her hand subsided.

He looked at her in concern. ''You ought to have that looked at.''

''I'm fine. It was a stupid thing to do.'' She was surprised to find his arms around her. Even more surprising was the fact that she didn't want to move out of their circle of warmth. The love she'd tried to banish could no longer be denied.

Clint, too, wore a bemused expression. ''I'm glad you're all right.''

She couldn't help the tiny moan of contentment that fell from her lips. It felt so good, so right. She snuggled against him and inhaled deeply of his tangy scent.

''It's been so long,'' he murmured, her hair muffling his words.

''So long,'' she echoed.

Unwilling to let her go, he led her back to the living room. He looked in distaste at the hideous couch.

She followed his gaze. ''Pretty awful, isn't it?''

"Yeah." He lowered her gently, searching her face for the answer which could end his torment.

"Brittany, I love you. If I have to spend the rest of my life proving it to you, I will. But I hope you'll believe me now, because I don't want to waste another minute without you and Andy." He waited for the most important answer in his life. It came.

"I love you. I've loved you almost from the first. I hated myself for sending you away." She nestled further into his arms.

His arms tightened around her. "Not half as much as I hated myself." Dark shadows beneath his eyes betrayed the sleepless nights he'd spent thinking of her, wanting her, praying for the chance to be part of her life again.

She smoothed the lines grooved around his mouth. The weeks apart had taken a toll on him as they had on her.

He rained tiny kisses along her brow, her eyes, her cheeks, finally finding the soft sweetness of her mouth. Her lips parted, opening in surrender to the feelings she'd dammed up for too long.

When he raised his head, he looked at her in wonder. "You love me." Only now did her earlier words penetrate.

"Yes. I love you."

"Then why did you send me away?"

"I thought you felt guilty. Or sorry for me and Andy. I didn't want your pity or your guilt. That's no way to start a marriage."

He looked genuinely perplexed. "Why would you think that? I asked you to marry me."

"Do you remember what you said after you asked me?"

His brow creased. "I think I said I loved you."

She shook her head. "You said you wanted to *take care of Andy and me*. You didn't mention love once."

His face cleared in understanding. "Oh, Brittany, what you must have gone through. Like an idiot, I thought you knew. I thought the whole world could tell I was crazy in love with you."

He kissed her again, more deeply this time, before reluctantly releasing her. Crossing the room, he picked up his jacket. He slipped a hand into his pocket and withdrew a small velvet box.

She held her breath. It couldn't be.

In two quick strides, Clint was once more at her side. He knelt beside her and, opening the box, withdrew a simple gold band and slid it onto her finger. "I know this isn't the proper way. There should be soft music and wine and all that. But I mean it more than I've ever meant anything in my life. Brittany, will you marry me?"

Tears pricked her eyes. "Pretty sure of yourself, weren't you?" she asked, talking around the lump in her throat, unable to take her eyes from him.

His lips slanted into a smile. "I had a long talk with Andy the other day. He made me think there was still hope."

"How does he know so much? He's only six."

Clint grinned. "He's one smart little guy. I hope an old man like me can keep up with him. Now, are you going to make me stay down here all night or will you give me an answer?"

She cocked her head to the side, studying him. "I think I like you on your knees."

"Brittany—"

"I'll marry you. Wherever and whenever you say." The words felt right. So right she wanted to shout them to the world. Instead, they were whispered between soft gasps.

"My wonderful Brittany. Don't ever change that sweet honesty of yours." With his arms around her, he kissed her. "I love you."

"And I love you. Whether you're a handyman or company president, I love you."

"I'm neither one now."

"I don't understand."

"I've turned the business over to my foreman. He'll run it for me. I'll have to sit in on a few meetings, but that's about all."

"What will you do now?"

"I've started another business."

"What kind of business? Maybe I could help."

"That's what I was counting on. I've been thinking that I want to give something back. I've been a taker for too long."

"You're not a taker or a user. You're gentle, kind, and loving."

He kissed her. "You're prejudiced." He took her

hands in his. "One time you told me about your dream—a center for families with special-needs children. I've been thinking about that a lot. Actually, I've been doing more than thinking." Quickly he outlined his plans for the Rainbow Children's Center.

"The Rainbow Children's Center," she repeated softly. "I like it. I like it a lot."

"I hoped you would."

"It won't be easy," she warned. "There'd be all kinds of red tape, rules and regulations you'd have to follow, finding the right teachers, plus getting the families to admit they need help. That's the hardest part of all."

"Are you trying to talk me out of it?"

"No! I just want you to know what you're getting into."

"I can't do it alone," he said, looking at her. "I'd need the right partner."

She dared a glance up at him. "Do you have anyone in mind?"

"I might." An answering glint lightened his eyes. "I just might." He sobered. "Together, we could make the dream come true. You and Andy and me." He fitted a finger under her chin. "I still believe in happily-ever-afters and rainbows. How about you?"

Love shone from her eyes. "I never stopped believing. Only I got lost along the way." She brought his hand to her lips and kissed his palm. "I'm not lost anymore."

Epilogue

Clint waited outside Andy's room while Brittany and her parents enjoyed their reunion. Laughter was interrupted by occasional tears. He wanted to be a part of it, but knew Brittany needed this time with her parents and Andy to herself.

The door opened.

While Brittany made the introductions, Clint felt himself being openly scrutinized by her father, a thin man in a red flannel shirt and well-worn jeans. Brittany's mother subjected him to a more subtle, but no less thorough examination.

"We'll see you back at the apartment," her mother said to Brittany with a meaningful look directed at Clint.

"Okay."

Brittany and Clint visited Andy together.

"Did you meet my grandparents? Aren't they cool?" Andy asked of Clint.

"They sure are." Clint looked at Brittany, who gave him a faint nod and smile. "How'd you feel about adding a new member to the family?"

Andy frowned. "Who?"

"Me."

"You? You mean you'd live with us all the time?"

"All the time."

"And we could go fishing, and play ball, and all that kind of stuff?"

"We'd do all the stuff you want," Clint promised.

A wide grin split Andy's face. "I say yes."

Clint cleared his throat. "I was hoping you'd feel that way. As soon as you're out of the hospital, your Aunt Brittany and I are going to get married. I'd like you to be my best man."

Andy turned to Brittany. "You hear that? Clint wants me to be his best man." He paused. "What's a best man do?"

"He's the groom's right-hand man. So that means you have to do it because you're already my number one helper."

They stayed until Andy fell asleep. Together, they walked outside.

Clint looked up, the rain having given way to a drizzle. Sun nudged its way through the mist. "Look."

She saw it. A rainbow arched across the sky, its colors clear and radiant, dispelling the veil of clouds. She put her hand in Clint's.

"Let's go home."